LIGHTS

ZUZANNA BLASZCZAK

INFINITY
PUBLISHING

Copyright © 2015 by Zuzanna Blaszczak

ISBN 978-1-4958-0613-1

This is a work of fiction. Names, characters, places, and incidents either are the product of the author's imagination or are used fictitiously. Any resemblance to actual events or locales or persons, living or dead, is entirely coincidental.

Published June 2015

INFINITY PUBLISHING
1094 New DeHaven Street, Suite 100
West Conshohocken, PA 19428-2713
Toll-free (877) BUY BOOK
Local Phone (610) 941-9999
Fax (610) 941-9959
Info@buybooksontheweb.com
www.buybooksontheweb.com

PROLOGUE

A short, stout man paced back and forth in his dark office, considering. He heard a knock on his dark red door over the rumbling and creaking of the Generator behind the back wall of his office and looked up sharply. The man quickly snapped his fingers and he grew–shapeshifted–to a tall young man with a handsome face and a comb-over. He took a seat behind his desk and clasped his hands together.

"Come in," he called in a deep voice. The door opened and a military soldier in a camouflage suit walked in and carefully closed the door behind him.

"Afternoon, sire," the soldier politely replied and bowed his head to the man.

"Is it afternoon already?"

"Yes, sir."

"What happened today? Did anybody find out about my 'gift' yet?"

"No, sir."

"Then what happened?" The man impatiently twiddled his thumbs while his hands rested on the desk, urging the soldier to go on.

The soldier looked nervous as he responded, "We caught the person you wanted us to capture, sir."

"Ah." The man looked happy. Relieved even. "Cody Dalton Vares?"

"Yes, sir."

"Please, call me James–" The man winked at the soldier– "Captain Mascao Judah Ingalls." And the soldier knew that that was the Elector President's name when he shape-shifts to his original stout body of his.

Mascao made a frightened look on his face as the Elector laughed. "You know, that Cody knew we were going to do 'it'." The soldier nodded at the Elector, and watched as he snapped his fingers once more. He shifted back to his small, chubby size and the soldier nodded again.

"I know, James."

PART 1
CRIMINALS

CHAPTER 1

Cody woke up and groaned. He'd been having a really strange dream about being in a room with sterile white walls, Executioners, and a shot. *Thank God it's over*, Cody thought and opened his eyes. Blinding, white lights glared at him and Cody quickly squeezed his eyes shut. *Uh oh*, Cody thought to himself again and slowly opened his eyes one more time. The light made his head ache, so he just kept his eyes closed. Where was he? What was he doing here? Not ready to face the situation, Cody pretended he was still asleep.

Cody racked his brain trying to remember what happened. He was at the air bus stop when an old man approached him and whispered to him, "Run, boy, run!" Cody figured the man was disturbed but when his air bus came, two men in silver suits stepped off and started to walk straight at him. Right when they were about to get to him, Cody realized he should've done what the old man had told him to do, but it was too late by then.

He rolled over on his side and opened his eyes again. He was still in the same room with sterile white walls. There were no doors, nor were there any windows. There was just him, the blinding, glaring lights, and the bed he was laying down in.

Then suddenly Cody realized what he was doing here. He was being Executed.

Why was he going to be Executed? What did he do wrong? Cody sat up and hopped off of the bed.

The room was an 8x8 square foot room—pretty small for an Operation Room. Everything in the Operation Room was white. Clearly the Executioners were going to store away the room so they could leave Cody's body there.

Cody was strolling around the tiny room when suddenly a wall slides open and an Executioner comes in with a clipboard. He had dark hair with a buzz-cut and he had dark skin. When he stepped in, the door closed firmly. Probably so Cody won't escape. Cody decided to speak up.

"What am I doing here?!"

The Executioner just chuckled and slapped down the clipboard onto his thigh. "You'll find out soon enough."

Cody shuddered as a shelf pulls out from the side of his bed and the Executioner opened a drawer and places the clipboard in, taking out a TouchPad. He started to type in some things. Cody figured that he was typing: *Subject replies in aggressive way. Subject was found walking around room.*

With his hands curled into fists, Cody walked back to his bed and sat down. "What did I do? Did I commit a Crime?"

The Executioner's mouth twitched as he pulled out another syringe from a drawer. Cody slowly backed away on his bed as the Executioner smiled and squirted little drops of liquid sleeping tablets.

Then, the Executioner held down Cody against the bed as he struggled against his grip, inserted the syringe quickly into Cody's arm, and the world went blank.

Cody woke up with people talking. He listened, but he still pretended to be asleep.

"Should we Execute him?" Cody heard someone say. He shivered at the word "Execute". He wasn't ready to face death. Yet.

"Hmm…Well, he *has* committed a Crime…" Another voice said, trailing off. Cody? Committing a Crime? What did he do?

Suddenly he was up. "What did I do? Have I been out at curfew? I don't remember being out at curfew-" Cody stopped himself. He wasn't in the Operation Room anymore. He was in a small office, even smaller than the Operation Room. He was sleeping in a bunk that was attached to the wall of the office. There were two people in the room talking to each other, a man and a woman. The man was the Executionist. He was changed into a silver, gleaming suit, with his dark, smooth hair combed over. The woman was wearing a blood-red dress with midnight black high heels with a jean jacket draped over her shoulders. Her greasy, black hair was in a ponytail, the way all women and girls should have. They stopped chattering and stared at Cody, their faces full of confusion.

The Executionist began talking. "Ahem, Cody Dalton Vares, you have committed a Crime, and we shall continue your Execution."

Cody's face flushed with anger. "I. Didn't. Commit. A. Crime. Where's my lawyer?! You people are disgusting!"

The woman continued for the Executionist, "You have been out in public without your uniform."

Cody was stunned. He has been out without his uniform? In the Government, the rules were that children must wear their uniforms for school and coming back from school. Cody was out at the air bus stop without his uniform because he just came back from school and was merely going to the store for groceries.

"I know," Cody responded instead, "I was going to the store to retrieve groceries, and I was already back from school."

The woman was not finished talking. "There are new rules in the Government now." She stood up, and with everyone staring at her, she walked over to the desk that was standing next to Cody's bed and slid open a drawer. She pulled out a roll of paper and walked back to her seat, opening the roll of paper.

"The Rules of the Government," she read.

"The Rules of the Government

1: All women and girls shalt have their hair up.

2: Pupils must wear their uniforms at all times in public.

3: Pupils must have proper education and go to school.

4: All children in the year of 15 must attend the Matching Ceremony.

5: All residents of the Government shall not be out of their homes from 10:00 pm to 5:00 am.............."

Cody knew this was going to go on for a long time. The Rules of the Government are endless; the Government is always adding more and more rules that all of the children at school need to learn and memorize. Cody memorized already over 100 rules of the Government in school. He remembered the time at school once he took a test of all the Rules so far. Cody knew that the woman was going to endlessly read all of the rules, and he already memorized them, except for the new one, and Cody could already see that the Executionist's head was bouncing down and jerking back up; obviously he was trying not to fall asleep.

By the time the woman got to Rule number 43, Cody stopped her. "Okay, I get it. I memorized all of those a long time ago…"

"But this is the updated version of the Rules of the Government," she said matter-of-factly. "You should be able to know this version. You must have learned it in school."

"The schools didn't get the updated version yet," Cody replied, trying to keep his temper. This woman was giving Cody such a hard time, of course he didn't learn the new rule in school yet. If the Government printed out the new version a week ago, then the schools would probably get their copies of the Rules two weeks later.

"Can we just change the subject?" Cody asked, tired of talking about the Rules. "If the Government printed that out a week ago, then of course I wouldn't know that I should be walking around with my uniform in public all the time!"

"Hmm… Alright… Let me check the Information…" the Executioner said, pulling out a TouchPad. "Says here…" The Executioner tapped a couple of times on the shiny, smooth screen of the TouchPad while Cody and the woman sat and waited. "Ah!" The Executioner turned the TouchPad around for everyone to see. "Turns out that the schools *didn't* get the updated version yet!"

Cody breathed a huge sigh of relief. So he didn't break the Rules! Cody felt that a huge weight has been taken off of his shoulders. He doesn't need to be Executed! Cody did a happy dance in his mind and smiled a little.

"Wait, wait, wait…" the woman said that made Cody worry again. "That Information is from two and a half weeks ago!"

The Executionist looked confused at first, but then he scrolled down a little bit more on the TouchPad. Then his eyebrows raised. "Ah! You're right! Cody, we will have to continue your Execution, due to our honest mistake."

Due to their honest mistake?! Cody felt faint. Today, he would have to die. Cody didn't want to die just yet. He wanted to have a Pair, go on with life, have a good education.

Then suddenly Cody remembered the invisible pill he still had in his Pill Box. While the Executionist and the woman were planning Cody's Execution, Cody silently slipped out his Pill Box from his jeans pocket and flipped it open. There were four Pills. The blue one was the sleeping pill, the red one was the calming pill, the yellow one was the survivor's pill, and last but not least, the green one was the invisible pill.

Cody has never used any of the pills before unless he had an absolute emergency.

Now he was going to use the one he always wanted to use.

Cody's plan was to take the invisible pill, and slip under the bed. The Executionist and the woman won't be able to see him, and they would think he was escaped. They would go out of the room, and then Cody would have his chance to escape.

He just hoped all of this would work.

Invisible pills last for five hours, which would give Cody just enough time to do his thing. Cody squished his eyes shut, sent a prayer to Nobody in particular, and placed the pill in his mouth.

The invisible pill dissolved in his mouth, and a salty flavor slid down his throat. Then, almost immediately, Cody couldn't see his hands.

Cody smiled to himself and slid under the bed, hoping somebody would notice him gone.

Then, as if right on cue, the Executionist turned his head towards the bed, and his eyes turned as wide as saucers as he noticed Cody's disappearance.

"Uh...Julie?" the Executionist asked anxiously. The woman stopped talking and faced the Executionist's direction. Then she glanced at the bed and her eyes also turned wide.

"He–he's gone!" Julie exclaimed. "But how–?"

Julie and the Executionist frantically looked around the room and rushed out the door, leaving murmurs and exclamations behind them.

Cody heard the room go silent, and cautiously peeked out from under the bed. To his amazement, no one was there, and Cody happily pushed out from under the bed and slipped out the door.

He was in a long, narrow corridor full of portraits of famous people of the Government, with the floor covered with a red velvet carpet. The corridor was dimly lit, which made it hard for Cody to see. He shuffled down the corridor, hoping he was going towards the exit, without making a sound. Whenever he heard something creak, he would hold his breath and realize that the creaking was him. After about seven creaks and breath holding, Cody found out that he was the only one in the long, dark corridor.

Soon after what it felt like hours to Cody, he finally found a dead end where there was a cedar wood door with a silver doorknob.

Cody reached out for the doorknob and prayed that no one was on the other side. He slowly twisted the doorknob and pushed open the door.

Sunlight made his eyes water and when his eyes finally adjusted, Cody saw that he was in a room with a lot of windows and there was a desk with a woman in wire-rimmed glasses typing away on a TouchPad.

Cody figured that the woman didn't notice Cody slipping past her desk and out the door.

The sun made his face warm and Cody was grinning ear to ear. He was free. He couldn't believe he just escaped from Execution, but he knew then that his life was in jeopardy.

CHAPTER 2

C ody burst inside his house just after the invisibility pill wore off and found everyone sitting at the dining table, worrying about Cody's disappearance.

He immediately noticed his mother, who looked the most worried.

"*Where were you?!*" she asked frantically. "We've all been so worried!"

Cody's mother's eyes were so wide that Cody thought they were going to pop out of her skull. She stood up and rushed over to squeeze Cody into a hug, followed by his two sisters, his father, and his grandmother following along.

"Tell us everything," Cody's sister, Jade, told him. Everyone else was agreeing with Jade, and stared at him urgently.

So Cody told them. He told them about how he was caught and was supposed to be Executed, how he didn't know that he was supposed to wear his uniform at all times, and how he escaped.

His grandmother's mouth was open when he finished, and she said, "Oh, this is bad. This is very, very bad…" She was lost in her thoughts when his father spoke up, "Cody, were you not paying attention in school?"

Cody thought this question over. He didn't remember learning this new rule in school yet. Obviously the Government was up to something.

"Father…" Cody said, seating himself at the table with everyone staring at him. "I always pay attention in school. I don't remember learning this new rule."

Cody looked around his terrified family. His grandmother was lost in thought, his two sisters Jade and Crystal were shaking violently with eyes wide, his father looked very urgent and worried, and his mother looked the most terrified.

His father sighed. "That would only mean one thing." He sat down and exhaled heavily, putting his hand on his forehead in exasperation.

"What?" Cody asked, straining his neck to get a good look at his father.

Cody's father was one of the all-day-work fathers. He was still in his Uniform with his tie untied, but not completely. Like all men at work should have, Cody's father also had a comb-over, but his chestnut brown hair was ruffled, and it barely looked like a comb-over anymore. Cody knew his father was tired, so he sat politely and waited for an answer while his father was trying to get over it.

"It…Means…" Cody's father trailed off and kept Cody waiting, and he finished with a sigh, "You have committed a Crime."

"Father," Cody replied, "I know."

Cody stopped talking and fell silent, gazing up at his family.

"I know."

The next day, when it was still dark and the sun hasn't risen yet, Cody's family was sleeping soundly while Cody wouldn't sleep. He kept wide awake all night, and he was exhausted. But whenever he closed his eyes and tried to sleep, the image of Execution came back, and Cody would snap back awake.

He didn't know what would happen to him. Cody still couldn't believe he escaped, and he couldn't get it out of his head.

Finally, after a lot of tossing and turning, Cody fell asleep.

He dreamed that he was back in the Operation Room, and there was the Executionist, his dark skin slick with sweat. He started walking towards Cody, and he quickly hid his face. But the

Executionist walked right past him and to a dull steel chair where sat a figure Cody couldn't quite recognize. Then the Executionist started to talk to the figure sitting on the chair.

"I know, you have gone through so much…"

"Don't talk about it," the figure told him, and the Executionist fell silent.

"What do we do?" the Executionist whispered, bringing the clipboard he was clutching in his hands to his fuzzy not-yet-shaved chin.

"Send him to Poverty," the figure replied, shooing the Executionist off and putting his hands on his head, crouching over and setting his elbows on his knees.

"A-As you wish, James," the Executionist said softly, looking down with the clipboard still under his chin, and slowly backing away toward the wall.

James, James. Cody knew the name sounded familiar. And the voice. The wonderful, soothe voice, heavy but gentle like honey…

That's it. James!

"Who is it," Cody demanded suddenly, standing up sharply from his corner and walking to James, "that you are going to send to Poverty?"

James and the Executionist looked both shocked and appalled to see Cody standing there demanding an answer from an oh-so familiar person named James.

"Why," James started to speak, letting out a nervous chuckle, "I never noticed young Cody Dalton Vares here in this very room." James stood up, and Cody realized this was not a familiar man at all.

This was a short and stout man, small for his age, and had wrinkles on his forehead, and a comb-over over his forehead on his head. Cody was pretty sure the comb-over was fake, and was just a wig, and wigs are forbidden in the Government, because the forward part of his so-called hair was tipping off over his head and onto his forehead, where he reached out with his hand to brush it out of the way.

Cody stilled glared at James, waiting for an explanation, with his hands crossed over his chest.

"Alright, Cody," James started, "I guess you deserve an explanation. We are, indeed, sending you to Poverty, which is on the other side of the Wall, where you will be sent with one bottle of water, one knife, and one box of saltines, where you are going to fight to the death with about a dozen and a half more Criminals like you. We are doing this for your own good, Cody–" James paused for a second to glance at Cody's expression– "Because the Government would not like any Criminals lurking about our beloved grounds." James ended his lecture with a mighty puff of triumph.

Cody stood there devastated, with absolutely nothing to say at all. He opened his mouth, and closed it, and repeated this several times with nothing to say for a minute of silence with James and the Executionist staring at him when he finally whimpered, "But I didn't know I did something wrong!"

"Ah," James said, "indeed you haven't. But remember when you, hmm, I don't know, *escaped* from Execution? Oh, I'm sorry, but maybe you didn't *know* you did this!" And finally James finished with a last sentence that changed Cody's life: "You know, you cannot change the past, but you can prepare for the future."

As the dream faded out, and Cody thought back to what James said to him at the end. "You cannot change the past, but you can prepare for the future."

Cody thought about his dream for a moment, for it was a dream like no other, and finally he realized it and always has realized it: The Government was up to something.

Cody woke up with the soft pattering of rain outside. He groaned and looked over his side to look out the window to see that it was pouring rain, with the gutters of the houses overfilled with water and the ground soggy. Cody threw off his blanket pushed his legs over the side, sitting up and wiping the sleep out of his eyes. He looked down at his bare legs, white shorts, and long red denim shirt he sleeps in. Cody stood up and shuffled over to his bathroom, switching the lights on. He went to the sink and pulled the lever to turn on the water, and scrolled the little button next to the lever down to make the water cold. He cupped his hand, let them run under the water, filling his cupped hands up, and splashed the water across his face. Dazzled, Cody's mouth dropped open, breathing heavily. He backed away from the sink, switching off the water, and flapping his hands. He grabbed the towel nearest him and dried his face and hands. And then he left to bathroom to leave his room.

When he got to the kitchen, Cody pressed a couple of buttons on the wall right to him. Then from the wall behind the counter slid out a bowl, a spoon, and some milk and cereal. Cody went to pour the milk into the bowl and then twisted the cap shut and placed it back in the hole in the wall. Then he grabbed his bowl, spoon, and cereal and made his way to the table to have breakfast.

Cody was about halfway through his breakfast when he heard the padding of someone's footsteps and looked up to see his sister, Jade.

"Hey," she said to him and pushed a couple of buttons on the wall next to her followed by fresh toast and jam sliding out of the hole in the wall. Jade walked over and clutched the plate of toast in her hand, strolling over to the chair next to Cody and sat down, putting the plate down on the sleek granite table counter.

"Hey," Cody replied casually after swallowing a spoonful of cereal.

"So what do you think will happen now?" Jade asked Cody, looking at him with wide curious eyes and taking a bite of toast.

"I dunno," Cody mumbled, looking down and upset that his sister asked him that after all he's been through.

Jade noticed how he turned his head on her and said, "Oh, sorry. I'm just scared."

Not as scared as I am, Cody thought gloomily, sipping the last drop of milk in his cereal bowl and returning the bowl and cereal back in the hole in the wall. Then he walked right past Jade and into the family room.

Cody sat down on the plaid couch and stared at the black television until he heard a faint knock on the door.

Jade also heard the knock, because she perked up and said, "Let's go see who it is."

Cody knew that he was twelve years old, and his little sister was ten, but he was trembling with fright while Jade confidently shuffled to the door and opened it. On the other side of the door stood another man in a silver suit, a comb-over, and dark shades with his hands behind his back.

"Oh, hi," Jade began cheerfully. When the man didn't respond, she looked over his side and said, "Helloooooo? Is anyone there?"

Cody got to the door just in time to stop Jade from waving her arms in front of the man's face, and he realized he made a mistake of coming there.

"Good morning," the man finally announced in an unemotional tone, without making any facial expression. Cody shooed off his sister and stood by the door, clutching the door so hard his knuckles turned white.

"Hello," Cody answered in his Southern accent, his voice cracking. Cody hoped that the man didn't notice his voice cracking.

When the man continued, Cody went on breathing again when he found out that apparently the man didn't notice. "Are you Cody Dalton Vares? Or do you have him in your household?"

Cody froze and hesitated, searching for a lie.

"No…" Cody said slowly, looking around the background of the man. "Cody Vares lives in the house across. We go to school, but we hardly know each other."

"All right, then," the man replied. "Good day."

Cody breathed a huge sigh of relief as he closed the door, and he walked into the family room giddily.

"So, what happened, Mr. Happy-Liar Pants?" Jade teased, turning over on the couch.

Cody grumbled and stumbled over to Jade, slumping on the couch. He heard some other soft padding of footsteps down the hall and he looked up to see Crystal, her thumb in her mouth on one hand and a plush teddy bear in her other hand dragging across the floor. She was only a toddler, in her pink bunny-rabbit pajamas and her ruffled blonde hair, but she had an eidetic memory, and knew how to talk perfectly. She even remembered the day she was born, and what she wore for her first birthday.

"Hi, Cody," she mumbled through her thumb. "Can I have a stool?" She pops her thumb out, wiping it on her pajamas and looks up into the air dreamily. "Interesting fact about stools, they were first invented in 1410 by a Swiss woman named Maria…"

"Ok," Jade pipes up. "Enough with 'fact time'. This is weird. How are you not worried? Yesterday Cody escaped from Execution!"

Cody felt his stomach drop to the ground as Crystal began with a new fact.

"Interesting fact about Execution, it was founded by a man named Julius Black from San Francisco, California, in 2030…"

Jade and Cody covered their ears and groaned. It was fun to have a little sister that remembers everything she's seen, read, thought, or heard, but if she keeps talking about "interesting facts" with everything people come up with, then she becomes annoying.

Cody got up, remembering why Crystal started talking in the first place, and walked to the hole in the wall, pressing a button, and a sippy cup with warm light brown apple cider slid out, and Crystal grabbed it, flipping open the lid and sipping the apple cider thoughtfully. "I'm too old for sippy cups, Cody," she gurgled through the cider and swallowed. "You should know that."

"You're only two years old, Crystal," Cody replied. "You could spilled something or whatever."

Crystal harrumphed and sat down on the couch, switching on the TV. She grabbed the remote and switched channels until she landed on the news channel. Cody blinked as they talked about a notorious Criminal wanted in the Los Angeles. On the bottom of the screen was a line rolling from left to right that said "Wanted dead or alive! 300,000 Book reward Cody Dalton Vares."

Cody couldn't believe it. He was a wanted Criminal dead or alive for a 300,000 Book reward.

Cody stared at a woman with a brick red jacket and a black plaid skirt with her hair down, as only news reporters would have to make an impression on TV. "Notorious Criminal Cody Dalton

Vares wanted after escaping slyly from Execution. Examiners have checked the entire office he was last in, only to find a drop of green on the white carpet, proving that he escaped using the invisible pill. The Elector President has been decided with the Senate that, invisible pills are now banned in the Government. Cody wanted dead or alive for a reward of 300,000 Books. I'm Sarah Von Tribuette, and that's it for this morning's news. Good morning, Government! And now for the pledge."

Cody's mind was racing so fast that he clutched his head in anticipation. He knew that he escaped Execution, and that is the number one law in the Government, but he never learned the new rule in school. He always paid attention to class and the teacher's smooth voice. He enjoyed listening to Mrs. Blue, his favorite teacher's voice. Smooth as honey, silky as, well-silk! He shook his head and peered out of the window next to the door. There were *swarms* of jet black cars parked around the neighborhood with similar men in silver suits walking from door to door, looking. For him.

CHAPTER 3

A pril sat on the couch curiously watching the news with Sarah Von Tribuette announcing the news about Cody Dalton Vares, the Government's new, most notorious criminal after escaping Execution. She looked down at her thin black shirt, washed so many times that it turned white and very thin at the edges. She stretched out her legs on the couch and lounged back as Whiskers, her mischevious tabby cat jumped onto her, asking to be petted. April scratched her head and Mascao, her older brother, walked in with a plate of bread and jam. Ever since her parents died, Mascao has been taking care of her, being twelve years older than she.

"Hey, Mascao," April piped up, "can you tell me why my name's April again?"

April always loved to ask this question, even though she always knew the answer. When she was little, just out of curiosity, she once asked Mascao why her name was April.

"Because," Mascao began with little April sitting enthusiastically on his lap just waiting for the answer, "there's this rhyme that's based on something real in life: April showers bring May flowers. Which means, your showers bring light and magic in our lives, just like the showers in April bring the flowers in May."

But what Mascao answered to April was not what she had expected.

"Not today, April."

That's when April figured something was very wrong.

April grabbed her backpack designed with cats and stripes and flew outside in the warm spring air. It was the month April, and it was her favorite month ever. In April, yes, there is rain, but there are always birds chirping and the sun shining and rainbows stretched out across the sky. She made a turn and walked with a skip in her every step as she made her way to the Hub for her breakfast. April listened to the jingles of coins in her pocket and opened the door to the Hub.

Immediately April heard soft chattering and small commotion in the Hub as people talked about politics, the Government, the people, and, most of all, about Cody.

April sat down on the nearest seat and slid off her backpack, placing it on the seat next to her.

"Hey, hey, hey." The voice could not belong to anyone else but Rocky, April's best friend. April looked up to see Rocky standing behind the counter, pouring some lemonade into a glass for her.

"Hey," April replied, and fell silent, taking the glass of lemonade and sipping on it. Rocky stood for a moment, waiting for April to say something else "interesting". She rolled up her sleeves and put her elbows on the counter. "Soooo," she began, looking up to April.

"So," April said back to her, taking another sip out of the glass.

"Want the like?" Rocky asked, slipping out a pad and pencil, ready to take April's order.

"Yeah. And some chocolate chips."

"I knowwwwww," Rocky said in a singsong voice. April always ordered the same thing. Every day she went to the Hub for breakfast, and her favorite thing there was the chocolate chip pancakes. They were always so moist, and chocolatey, and sweet, and April adored them. Rocky worked at the Hub, and by the fifth day that April was there for the first time, Rocky memorized her orders. Rocky turned her back on April and started to prepare the ingredients for the pancakes. April waited a couple of minutes until she heard the sizzling of the pancakes. Rocky always worked fast on cooking, because she always knew what to do, and how to do it.

"Something happened," Rocky suddenly piped up as she flipped a pancake over in the air.

"How did you know?"

"April," Rocky started to say as she slid the last pancake on the plate and handed it over to April, followed by a fork, "we've been best friends since we were five. I think I know you by now."

April grabbed the fork and stuck it into the first pancake like a dagger, taking off a piece of the golden brown goodness and shoving it in her mouth. Chocolatey flavor exploded in her mouth and she chewed thoughtfully before answering to Rocky.

"Something's wrong with Mascao," she explained, taking another bite of the pancake.

"Like…"

April swallowed. "When I asked him why my name is April, he just shooed me off."

"Come on, dude," Rocky said and jumped onto the counter to sit on it. "Maybe he's just stressed out or whatever. And you asked him that question like a million times."

Rocky did have a point. "Huh. Maybe you're right, Rocks. He does have work today. And as a twelve year old, I need to take responsibility and suck it up."

"Yeah!" Rocky shouted, making people look. She leaned forward over the counter and gave April a mini noogie, almost knocking over the plate of pancakes. April coughed and gave Rocky the stink eye.

"Excuuuuuse me," she said with a smirk, "I'm tryin' to eat. I could choke, and you would have to do the Heimlich Maneuver on me."

Rocky laughed and jumped back down. "Hey, yeah. But then it'll mean that I could hug you tighter."

Rocky's jokes always made April laugh, and as she laughed, Rocky laughed with her, and with all of the people in the Hub looking at the ecstatic girls, they laughed with them, and before April could find out why it was so loud, the entire Hub was laughing.

That's when April figured that nothing was wrong after all.

CHAPTER 4

C ody knew what he had to do. He quickly went to his two sisters watching a cartoon on TV and gathered them together as the cartoon still droned on.

"Jadeline," he began, "Crystalette." His two sister listened to him with frightened looks on their round faces. They knew that whenever their brother called them by their full names, then something bad was about to happen. "I am now a wanted Criminal," Cody continued, "and I have to leave you in order to keep you safe."

At first the sisters though that Cody was kidding around with them, that the Government was all a joke, and everything could go back the way things were in the twenty-first century, but with the serious look on Cody's face and his bright blue eyes hardening as he squeezed them together, Crystal and Jade realized that Cody would have to disappear in the shadows forever.

CHAPTER 5

Three years later...

I glance at the clock. In just ten and one fifth of a second the test would be over and the bell will ring, therefore; school will be over and I could make plans to hang out with Rocky at the Hub where she begins her after-school work hours. Rocky has worked at the Hub since she was at a very young age. I smile to myself as I think about Rocky's first day at work when we were both twelve years old. But smiling was a bad idea, or was it my body's idea? I hear the snap of a ruler against a desk and look up carefully to see Mrs. Von Tribuette scowling at me with her arms crossed and her bright red lipstick shining down at me. It's funny when you think about it, the old lady used to be really pretty as she reported news on the Government News Team. I remember her reporting the news about Cody Dalton Vares, the Government's most wanted Criminal. She's changed a lot over the past three years.

"April Ingalls," Mrs. Von Tribuette hisses at me, "why are you smiling? This is a school!"

I hear some snickering behind me and will myself not to laugh. Something tells me that this lady's got problems. Once she yelled at a boy in class for writing *her* name wrong on an assignment.

Luckily, the bell rings just as she's starting to chew me out, and I ditch my paper, quickly shove my pencil into my backpack, and take off flying out of class with the backpack thumping on my back. Just when I walk out of school I spot Rocky and run over to her.

"Hey, hey, hey," she chirps at me. That thing will never get old as long as Rochelle Elizabeth Dale lives.

"Hey," I reply, twirling the end of my side braid and flickering my eyes at her.

Rocky just laughs. "Somethin' tells me Tribby did her ol' stuff again." As she says this, she grabs my head and noogies me, her curls in the ponytail of her brown hair bouncing about. The bright blue tips of her hair glisten in the sun. I remember when she boasted to me that she wanted to paint her hair. I giggle and struggle to release myself from her grip. Soon we walk along the sidewalk passing identical brick houses, and Rocky asks me, "So what did she do this time?"

"Well," I explain, "I had a memory… a good memory, and I kind of smiled a little while we were taking the test, and she snapped that big dang ruler of hers and she came over to me and screamed, 'What are you smiling about?! This is a school!'" I mock Mrs. Von Tribuette in a witch's voice which sends Rocky cracking up.

"That woman is *crazy*…" she starts to say and trails off, looking to her side. "Oh! There it is, the ol' Hub. C'mon."

With Rocky pulling me by the arm, we cross the street and walk into the Hub, where there a small group of people are sitting at the counter chatting about something or other, probably about Cody's latest scheme: blowing up a row of airships at the military base.

Rocky plops her backpack on a chair and goes to the other side of the counter where she grabs an apron and ties it on. I sit down on another chair and take out my folder, placing it on the counter and grabbing the pencil I ditched before. Then I put the backpack on the floor and get started on our math homework. I hear the frying of pancakes and look up to see Rocky slipping a third pancake on a plate with a fork.

"Thanks, Rock," I tell her and dig into the first pancake, forgetting about the homework. I'll do it later. When I'm finished eating.

"Hey," Rocky starts to say, "but it's gonna cost ya."

I don't know if she's serious or not, but I laugh anyway. I push the homework and folder to the side and listen to Rocky babble about her boy problems at school or whatever.

"Oh. My. God! In shooting practice, I swear, I think I caught Matt, ya know, Matt Fisher, like, staring at me! When I saw him, he was like, 'Whoops.' and his face got all red! I was trying not to laugh, because then, I'll, like, you know, snort, and then everyone in class would laugh at me and I hate it when people laugh at me because that means that they think that I'm weird, stupid, and just, like, weird, dude! Oh my goodness, I just realized! That if I get home from work late then Mom and Dad will take away my phone and without my phone I won't have a social life and without a social life then I won't have any friends, except you, right Appy? Well, anyway, when I won't have any friends then I will be sad and when I will be sad then I'll stop eating and when I stop eating then I'll get soooo skinny and when I'll be skinny then I'll be really light and when I'll be really light then people at school will think that I'm really easy to wrestle and when they think that I'm easy to wrestle then they'll wrestle me and when they'll wrestle me then I'll get hurt and when I'll get hurt then I won't be able to work here anymore and when I won't be able to work here anymore, well, then I won't have any money, and when I won't have any money, well, my life is, like, RUINED!"

Rocky ended this with a big gasp and I couldn't help but laugh so hard. Rocky always talks so much like this. Occasionally in huge cause-and-effect-mini-speeches like these.

"Calm down, girl," I try to soothe her. "Don't worry. I'm always here for you, no matter what. Okay?"

Rocky's breathing so hard right now. "Yeah. Okay."

I continue to eat my pancakes and everything's silent between me and Rocky when suddenly Mascao, dressed in a swamp green suit, bursts into the Hub.

"Emergency," he pants, "Cody has broken into the military Training Center. Everyone, as quickly as you can, leave and go to your homes!"

I want to ask him how and when he broke into the Training Center, but when he finishes, everyone starts bustling around, taking their belongings and Rocky rips off her apron, throwing it over to the side and she grabs her backpack just as I'm slipping a strap of mine on my shoulder. She grabs me by my arm and pulls me out of the

Hub, and we run together into the night toward our homes which are right next to each other.

When we reach them, Rocky gives me a quick salute and I salute back at her, and she makes a beeline for her house. I run over to the doorstep of my home and jiggle the doorknob at the front door.

The door is locked.

CHAPTER 6

T he Government has no idea what I'm doing.

I made a fake break-in at the military Training Center by sneaking in and throwing a pillow right in the middle of the hallway, which triggers the alarm.

I'm actually robbing houses. Pretty sneaky of me.

I've already broken into three houses. I could do better, but oh well.

This house that I'm in right now surprises me. Instead of jewels and the like sitting on shelves, I see gold trophies and ribbons piled on top of shelves, and it looks like the person who won these is captain of a military fireteam. There's nothing for me to see here.

Just as I'm making my way out of a window of the house, I hear the clinking of a doorknob.

Someone's already here.

Frantically looking left and right, I dash to the door, unlock it without making a sound, and race to the window jumping out. I land on the soft grass with a little thump and a little clinking of the valuables I have in my bag. I hold my breath, but apparently nobody heard me because somebody already switched on the lights in the house. I peek inside and see a girl with silky brown hair pulled back in a side braid with braces. I can see because she's looking at herself in the mirror. A cat lounges on the couch and the girl plops back, scratching the cat in the head. I don't know what I'm still doing here, but as I'm examining the girl, she turns out to be the coolest girl I've ever seen.

Her eyes flash olive green as she's laughing at a comedy show. Her cat backpack hangs on a hook near the door, and her hand with nails painted pink run over her cat's head.

I hear something behind me and yelp a little, turning around and quickly ducking down. A squirrel stares up at me with wide black eyes, standing on its hind legs.

"Scat, you," I mumble to the squirrel. The squirrel's nose twitches and it skitters away. I exhale and realize the girl's talking. I peek back through the window on my tippy toes, my black hair falling into my eyes. I brush them out of the way and listen to the girl.

"You're a cute bunny, yes you are!" the girl chirps at a black and white bunny she's holding in her arms. "Here, Oreo. You can play with Whiskers."

The girl sets Oreo on the ground and Whiskers hops (I know he's not a bunny. He literally hopped) over to Oreo and stretches out on his belly. Oreo lies down beside Whiskers and they cuddle together. It was the cutest thing I've ever seen.

"Nice cat," I say without thinking. A little bit too loud.

I hear the girl in another room. Man, I guess I've been paying attention so much to the cat and the rabbit that I didn't notice the girl leaving the living room.

"Mascao?" the girl says uneasily. "You there?" Her head pokes out of the other room and I quickly duck down. Oh, no. I think she saw me. I hear footsteps drawing closer and closer to the window...

"Who's there?" she asks and sticks her head out the window. I slowly look up with my hair in the way again and frown at her as she stares at me with terrified, wide eyes. She screams and ducks her head back in the window, and before I can escape, she's back again, only I see a glint of light in her hand. Oh, God. She's holding a knife.

"Cody," she growls through gritted teeth. I'm surprised she can recognize me in the dark, but I guess anyone can tell who I am with my freakishly bright blue eyes. I should really get colored contacts.

Or at least steal some. "Get away from my house, or I'm going to use this!"

The girl looks like she really isn't afraid to use the knife, so just like the squirrel, I skitter away into the dark.

CHAPTER 7

⸝⸝⸝⸝⸝⸝⸝

I can't believe that Cody has broken into my house.

I run over to the telephone that is installed in the wall and dial 9-1-1. The 9-1-1 number has been going on for hundreds of years.

"Hello, 9-1-1 at your service for emergency," a soft woman's voice says on the phone.

"Hi, my name is April Christina Ingalls, and I am the younger sister of Captain Mascao Judah Ingalls. I am reporting that Cody Dalton Vares has broken into my home. He has just left because I threatened him, so please warn the Elector President about this danger."

The woman laughs kindly and I blush with anger. "Oh, aren't you the cutest thing! All right, dear, I'll warn our glorious Elector President–"

"Lady," I growl, "there are people out there that may be in danger. If was trying to be cute, would I call 9-1-1?! This is a serious emergency system, and I am fifteen years old! Honestly, do you think I would try to be cute at a mature age?!"

Silence comes upon the end of the line. After five seconds of silence I respond. "I could call the Government Building and complain to the Senate of your negligence."

There is silence again until the woman suddenly pipes up, "All, right dear, I'll alert the Senate. Thank you for calling and have a nice night."

She hangs up and as I stand there with the phone still in my hand with the buzzing sound flowing through my ear, I realize that she isn't going to call the Senate.

I listen to the boiling water from the kitchen as I continue to watch a show on TV. Oreo hops onto the couch and squeezes in between me and Whiskers. I hug them together, shaking with fear and anger twisted with hope and relief. The show bores me and I shut it off. I sit silently with the boiling water dying down, and I hear the door open and close to my left. I see Mascao walk in, taking his cap off and kicking off his boots. I run over to him and hug him tightly. He hugs me back and tells me, "That was a long night. I'm proud of you keeping yourself safe."

I squish my eyes shut and let good memories flow in my mind. The time when Mascao took me out to try ice cream for the first time. When he took me to work. When we sat together on the very couch in the living room, talking about Mom and Dad.

Tears flood my eyes and I let myself sob. Mascao ruffles my hair and says to me, "I'm so glad you're safe, kid. But I can tell something happened."

I pull back and wipe my eyes, looking up at him. "Mascao... Cody wasn't breaking into the Government Building. He was breaking into houses. He broke into our house. But I scared him away. With a knife. I don't know where he is now. But I'm scared." I babble like a little kid to him and Mascao smiles sadly. He runs his hand through his hair and says, "Ok, April. Let's go eat and I can alert the Senate."

"But Mascao," I pipe up, "I already called 9-1-1. I told them everything, but they thought that I was trying to be cute." Tears spring into my eyes again and I collapse onto the couch with Whiskers and Oreo already perking up and running over to huddle against me. I can always count on them to cheer me up. I remember when I first got Oreo, followed by Whiskers. I was ten years old, and Mascao and I were at the pet store and I was pointing randomly at every animal I saw. Then finally I settled on a tabby cat with twitching whiskers and a black and white bunny with big, floppy ears and big, wide eyes staring up at me. I fell in love with both of them, and when we brought them home and set them together on the rug, Whiskers and Oreo already got along perfectly and immediately began to cuddle against each other.

I hear Mascao in the kitchen and I get up, steadying myself, and run over to him. He's pouring water into a cup with a tea bag, and plates are already set on the table filled with mashed potatoes and beets with broccoli.

In the Versa Sector, there are middle class people and they can prepare their own food. In the Poor Sector, families have to have dinner served from a couple of button-pushing and food sliding out from a hole in the wall. In the Diamond Sector, there are rich people who can afford servants, maids, and cooks.

I sit down at a chair and Mascao sets the cup of tea in front of me, and I begin to dig into the mashed potatoes and beets. I ignore the broccoli, pushing it out of the way. Mascao joins me on the other side of the table and sets a glass of milk in front of his plate.

Soon, the only thing I hear is the clinking of silverware against plates and the thumping of Oreo jumping around.

CHAPTER 8

I stay at the girl's house anyway. I overheard her talking to her brother, or dad, or uncle, or whatever, and found out that her name is April Christina Ingalls, and her brother's (or whatever!) name is Mascao Judah Ingalls, and that he's a military captain.

I also learned that she called 9-1-1 about me.

I shuffle through the bag that hangs on my side and take out a small rock. It could make a sound not too loud, and not too soft. I slip over to the window and watch Mascao walk upstairs. April is sitting on the couch with Oreo at her feet and Whiskers next to her. I think she's doing homework or something. I toss the rock at the glass, but not too hard, so the glass won't shatter. The rock makes a satisfying clicking sound and April immediately looks over her shoulder and gets up to see who made the sound. She opens the window and says, "Who's there?"

With me being well hidden in a dark shadow near the window, I respond, "It's me again, Cody."

I know I'm being stupid. Don't judge.

April yelps a little and glares at me. "Don't you have somewhere to be in the Poor Sector?"

This girl's hilarious. I give her a sly smile and reveal myself from the shadows. "Actually, yes I do, but ah, don't mind tellin' me where you got the hair, 'cause, uh, ya know-" I point to my hair and fluff it royally, "-I'm gettin' a haircut." My southern accent is really heavy, no matter how I try to hide it.

April does not look amused. "Okay, what do you want?" she snaps, literally snapping her fingers. Whiskers and Oreo perk up at the snapping and run over to April's feet.

I decide to tell her the truth with the night breeze flowing through my hair, making it get into my eyes again. "The truth is, I don't want to hurt you. I never wanted to hurt anyone. But, I have someone waiting for me, so I, uh, gotta go…"

"Wait." The sound of April's voice alarms me as I turn my back on her. I face her again and wait with my arms crossed. She said to wait, right?

"I have a deal for you," April continues as I listen to the song of frogs chirping. "If you will go away and leave me and my family alone, I won't report you."

That sounds like a great deal. I grin and take out my hand to shake hands with her, but she just stands there, scowling at me.

"I don't think I said this correctly," April says. "Go." She grabs the edges of the window, ready to close them. "Away." She slams the window shut which leaves me startled, and now, this time, I skitter away for good.

Chapter 9

The next morning is Saturday, which means I can sleep in. But instead, I get up early in my bunny pajamas and slip my feet into my cat slippers. (Funny thing is, it should be vice versa) I thump downstairs to find the house empty and quiet. I guess Mascao went to work early. I walk over to Oreo clattering in her cage and open the hatch. She jumps out and nudges me for food. I grab the bag of grains that was sitting on the cage and pour some into Oreo's bowl that sits next to the cage. With Oreo skipping over to the bowl and burying her nose in the food, I sit down on the couch and exhale deeply. I just don't understand why Cody came back last night. He doesn't do that to just anyone. What's going on?

My mind is whirring and I lay back on the couch and stare up at the ceiling until I hear knocking at the door. I get up, almost tripping over Oreo, and open the door. Rocky stands in front of me with a huge, toothy grin. She curled her hair today, and her brown curls are bouncing up and down. She's wearing pink sweatpants, bunny slippers, (ha) and a tank top with a baby blue baggy shirt over it.

"Hey, hey, hey," she squeals and rocks forward and back on her heels.

"Alright, what's going on?" I ask her suspiciously and push my hair out of my eyes. "You're not going to tell me something ridiculous, and you make me a promise and then we hug it out and I go into your little house on the prairie."

Rocky giggles hysterically and it makes me laugh too.

"Okay, seriously, Rocks," I tell her, "You sound like a squealin' guinea pig about to eat a pound of black eyed peas and kale with eggs sunny-side up."

Rocky giggles again and grabs my arm. "Hee, hee. C'mon, Appy. I have somethin' cool to show you."

I sigh and I close the door behind me, letting her pull me through the streets in the cool morning air in the summer. We laugh and run through the grass dressed with water drops until we're way out of the city and near the Wall. The grass here is the greenest green grass I've seen since India gained its independence. Daisies seep out of the ground and dandelion fuzz floats through the air. Since the Wall is glass, we can see boulders and old houses and more of the ripe, green grass. It's the most beautiful thing I've seen.

With my mouth open in awe, Rocky continues to pull me towards a tree that contains round, bright red balls that kind of look poisonous. Some of them are on the ground and little sticks stick out of them.

"Rocky," I whisper, "What is this?"

Rocky seats me beneath the tree and grabs one of the red balls and takes a big bite. I gasp as I stare at the pale inside with juice dripping out. Rocky laughs and grabs another one off of the ground, handing it over to me. "Try one. They're sweet. It's called an apple."

Apples. I take Rocky's offering and cup it in my hands. It feels smooth, and it looks poisonous. But since Rocky ate it and she's not dead yet, I should try. I take a big bite out of the apple and sweetness explodes in my mouth. It has its own taste, and its delicious. I wonder why the Government doesn't sell these anymore.

"Mmmm," I say as I take another bite. Rocky laughs again and as I keep taking bites out of the apple, Rocky whistles a cheery tune. I keep eating until I feel something hard. The apple's skinny, and there are black spots in the apple now. I squeak and throw it to the ground. Maybe those are the parts in the apple that are poisonous? I glance over to Rocky worriedly and she smiles at me as if I was a toddler taking her first steps.

"Don't worry, Appy," she tells me, "Those are seeds. You plant them in the ground for them to grow into another apple tree."

"Ohh," I breathe and take back the apple. I pick out one of the seeds and dig a tiny hole in the ground. I place the seed there and pad on some dirt into the hole. Then I sit back and wait.

After what it's been like five minutes I pipe up, "Why isn't the tree growing yet?"

Rocky responds to me soothingly, "That's because it takes some time to grow. About forty years, maybe."

"Oh. Okay." I get up and close my eyes, bringing my arms up to my sides as if I was an airplane. I run around aimlessly, not caring if I smash into something. I feel free. Like an animal. Or a squirrel. I laugh and Rocky laughs with me.

Suddenly I slam into something, and my eyes go wide from the stunning force as I roll backwards on the ground.

Now I do care what I smash into.

CHAPTER 10

"What are you doing here?" April demands, straightening her cat shirt. I lie back and hum carelessly.

"I asked you a question," April says and I sit up. She's standing with her arms crossed and her friend (or so I think) sits beneath the apple tree with a half-eaten apple in her hand. Her mouth is wide open with fright.

"I always come here," I respond to April and get up, busying myself with the strap on my bag. "And, uh, your friend over there is kinda scared."

April glances over her shoulder and runs from me to her friend. She kneels down and cradles her body to her. "It's okay, Rocky," she coos to her friend–Rocky.

I casually stroll over to the hugging girls and feel my face turn red. I try to hide it with a smirk.

"I saw you guys," I say to them, "and I decided to come and say hello."

April shoots me a disgusted look.

"So," I continue, "hello." Rocky and April get up and stand with their arms crossed. I hear birds chirping and bees buzzing. But I'm not finished talking. "Okay, the truth is… I notice very little people, April. And you're among, like, 1% of the Government that I notice."

April raises her eyebrows and looks over to Rocky. They both nod at the same time and start to walk away.

I harrumph a little and turn away from them, too.

Then I start to run.

I grab the ledge of a window at the nearest building and swing myself up onto it. I start to scale the building; maybe I'll get a better view of where Rocky and April are heading.

I climb past a man typing ferociously on a computer, so obviously he's too distracted to notice a 15-year-old boy with freakishly bright blue eyes and shaggy black hair scaling a 17-story building. I continue to climb until I reach the rooftop. I stand up and admire the view of the Government. I can see the towering building of over 100 stories high: The Government Building. The tower climbs way up above the clouds, and rumor has it that the Elector President has his office at the very top floor heavily guarded by 900 soldiers that were trained for half their lives.

For three years I have been wanting to break into the Government Building and find out what the Government is up to. That's because three years ago when I was twelve I was kidnapped by Government Agents and told that I committed a Crime. I was supposed to be Executed, but I escaped by using the one and only invisible pill that I had in my Pill Box. Then word spread out fast and the next day I was the Government's most notorious Criminal. I never understood why I was treated this way by the Government.

I scan the Government one more time and notice a little house in the Poor Sectors with a dim light.

My house.

CHAPTER 11

R ocky and I kick rocks and make jokes and laugh together as
we make our way to our houses to change. Rocky still kind
of looks mortified after seeing me casually talk to Cody, but I act
cool about it.

"What was that all about?" Rocky finally asks me after I make a
joke about tomatoes and ketchup.

"Oh," I say, "Well, it was that there were two tomatoes, and one
tomato ran ahead, and the second tomato said-"

Rocky cuts me off just when I'm about to get to the punchline.
"Yeah, yeah, I know. The second tomato said, 'You can go ahead, I'll
ketchup with you later!'"

I laugh hysterically at my own joke until I realize that Rocky's
serious. I stop abruptly and cough quietly.

"What I mean is," Rocky continues, "What was that all about
with you talking to–to–*Cody*. That was totally creepy, man."

I sigh and run a hand through my hair. "Okay, the thing is…
Cody broke into my house last night."

Rocky's eyes go wide as saucers. "He *what*?!"

"He broke into my house," I reply, running my fingers against
the glass Wall.

Rocky still looks devastated as we walk along the sidewalk of the
Versa Sector and we head separate directions to our houses.

When I open the door, Whiskers immediately greets me at my feet with a meow. I scratch his head and close the door behind me. I go into the kitchen and open the shades. The room floods with sunlight as I set the pot of water on the stove for it to boil. I make a beeline for the stairs and soon I come back downstairs into the kitchen with mismatched socks, not-too-skinny jeans, and a faded black shirt that says, "It's not easy being this cute!"

In the kitchen, I grab a mug and put a teabag in the cup. I pour the boiling water into the mug and take a spoon, stirring it in the tea.

Soon I'm back outside, sitting on a rocking chair on the porch in front of the front door. I sit back and watch the aircars float by as I sip my tea. Everything seems so peaceful as Whiskers marches over to me and curls up next to my chair. Since it's June, school ends soon. I wish every day was always like this, and that I never had that sinking feeling that the Government is up to something.

CHAPTER 12

I dash on rooftops of buildings and once in a while ducking down whenever someone or something walks by. I need to get to Jade and Crystal. They're the only people in my family that know I'm alive. The rest of my family doesn't know this because in the Poor Sectors, there are no JumboTrons displaying the news. The construction workers there just can't afford it. And also if people from the Poor Sector will travel to the Versa Sector or, even worse, the Diamond Sector, they will immediately be arrested and Executed.

I scan the horizon and swing down onto the ground from the back of a building. But I don't see my house at all.

The only thing that I'm staring at wide-eyed is the Execution Center, the place where I've began my life of Crime.

I decide to put on a disguise.

After rummaging a bit through my bag I find a notebook, a pen, some clothes, and a wig with red hair.

Soon I'm inside the Execution Center with my disguise.

I managed to find brown-eyed colored contacts, which beautifully hide my bright blue eyes. I put on the red-haired wig and on top of that I wear a gray news cap. I still have my bag, though, and in my hands I'm holding the notepad and pen, and I'm wearing a baggy bright blue shirt and brown sweatpants with sneakers.

I walk up to the lady that wears wire-rimmed glasses, typing away on the computer. I remember when I escaped from Execution three years ago I didn't even bother about the lady. But now I do need to bother her.

I stand before the steel desk while the sun flickers through the glass walls in the lobby of the Execution Center. I wait until there's a slight pause of the clacking, and I speak up.

"Um, excuse me," I say in my stupid Southern accent that'll definitely convince the woman to think that I'm the Government's most notorious Criminal. "I'm a news reporter in the *Daily Government* and I need to interview an Executioner. Can you set up an appointment?"

The woman looks up at me annoyingly from the computer and mumbles to me, "Mmm hmmm." I hear a couple of clicking until she finally replies, "Well, yes, I can set an appointment for you with Dr. Tyler Raven Black at six 'o'clock, is that alright?"

I glance at the (stolen) watch I wear at my wrist. It's two minutes until six. "Yes, that would be lovely. Thank you."

"Please take a seat while you're waiting," the woman tells me. She extends a hand towards the cushioned air-chairs that are lined along the glass windows. I sit down in one of the chairs and lie back. I order a coffee from the drink delivery in the armrest and sip it while I'm waiting for Tyler to come. The coffee will make me stay alert. For anything.

"Hello? Uh, I was set up for an appointment with… Annoying red-head?" a voice says questioningly from the door where I last was when I escaped Execution. So many good memories.

"Yes, that's me." I stand up with my coffee and raise my hand over my head.

"Yes, yes, that's good," Tyler mumbles to himself. He has dark skin, black hair, and he looks very young, maybe seventeen or twenty. And I realize that he's the Executionist who was going to perform my Execution.

I open a lid on a wall next to the door that's the trash. I feel the heat from the fire as I dump the empty coffee cup into the spitting flames. I turn back around and follow Tyler to the door.

When we're on the other side and everything's dark, Tyler tells me, "You can call me Ty. But I just have one question–why are you using a notebook and pen?"

Crud. One more mistake and I'm in the Operation Room. "Yes," I reply, my voice cracking the slightest bit, "I like to get in touch with the old-fashioned way of interviewing people. And also, I left my TouchPad at home."

Ty chuckles and opens another door on the side of the dark hallway. Light floods into the hallway and it makes me squint for having been in the dark for so long. When my eyes finally adjust, I see that I'm in a room with a black carpet, a cedar wood desk with a TouchPad sitting on it, and a window where I can see aircars passing by.

"Have a seat," Ty insists and gestures towards a dark red chair on the other side of the desk. I obey and plop down onto the chair, shifting into a comfortable position. I ready my pad and pen while Ty gets comfortable in his chair. I wait until Ty asks me, "So what's the first question?"

Oh, no. I haven't really figured out the questions yet. So I just try to wing it.

"So," I begin, "What really happened during Cody Dalton Vares's escape from Execution?" I scoot uncomfortably in my chair as Ty thinks through the answer to the question.

"Well, I was there." Ty strokes his chin in thought and continues, "He was in a room very far away from here, so he wouldn't escape that easily, because, it's really hard to find your way through there, right?" I nod, eager for him to go on.

"That room's under quarantine now," Ty finishes with a flick of his hand.

I study Ty more closely to find that he has a tattoo of a small black triangle on his collarbone. My father has that tattoo.

I hesitate a moment before continuing with the second question that pops into my head. "What do you think of Cody?"

Silence fills the room and suddenly I feel shy. I've never really asked anyone about this. Then Ty replies, "I dunno, it's kinda private."

I feel my face get warm and I stare down at my lap. I look back up to see Ty looking me over, considering me.

"Ok, then. I'll tell you," Ty says with a nervous laugh. He takes his hand and runs it over the back of his neck, over the triangle tattoo, anxiously. "So, the thing is, the Elector President. He... He makes Government Agents or soldiers capture the Disparate, ya know, the people who have a suspicion of him being evil. Ya know, when they do a brain scanning in the Versa and Diamond Sectors every month.

"Well, Cody lived in the Poor Sector, so he didn't get any brain scanning. But the kids in the Poor Sector go to school anyway, right? And you know that every school has Trials at the end of each year to test each student's IQ. And Cody's Trial Results came out different than everybody else's. The Senate studied the Results, and they settled to the decision of capturing him to Execute him.

"So you see, the Government doesn't want the people to think negative or suspicious thoughts about them. That's because they're planning something. But I cannot tell you what they are planning. So they Execute every person that has suspicions about the Government. When Cody was in the now-quarantined room, Dr. Juliette Harper Caprison and I told him that he committed a Crime and we created a little skit of pretending to search the Information on our TouchPad to get Cody to think that he really did commit a Crime, even though he didn't."

I didn't notice that my mouth went open while Ty was talking. I can't believe it. So the Government, or at least the Elector, *was* up to something!

And I'm going to figure it out.

Ty kind of laughed softly after he noticed me with my mouth open so wide that any moment now a fly would buzz inside there.

Suddenly I hear an ear-piercing alarm blare throughout the Execution Center and five military soldiers burst into the room and I jump out of my seat, and realized that Ty did too.

"Dr. Tyler Raven Black," a dark voice says out of nowhere, "You have been arrested for committing a Crime of telling too much Information."

I find myself screaming as they drag Ty out of the small office and the dark voice comes up again.

"And take the red-head for committing a Crime of knowing too much Information."

CHAPTER 13

S oon it's night, and Mascao is already home with his comb-over
ruffled up and his uniform covered with mud stains. I choose
not to talk to him because he looks like he's about to drop dead any
minute now.

I let Oreo back into her cage and I ponder upstairs with Whiskers
following along. In my bunny-themed room, I sit on the edge of my
bed with a light-pink quilt with an embroidering of a brown bunny
stretched back. Fluffy pillows with flowers on them perch next to
my window and an airchair floats behind my desk where I do my
homework. Whiskers hops into my bed next to me, and I want to
shoo him off, but I'm too lost in thought about Cody noticing *me*, of
all people. I stand up and walk over to the mirror planted on the wall
next to my desk and bare my teeth. My braces make my mouth look
huge, and my hair drapes over my eyes. My olive green eyes glisten in
the light that I turn on with two claps of my hands. I have two tiny
pimples on my forehead that I try desperately to hide with blush,
concealer, or even eyeshadow, but it never works. Mascao always
tells me to drink lots of water to prevent acne or to put an ice cube
on the zit.

But sometimes, I just don't feel like it.

I turn back around and plop onto my bed with Whiskers scatter-
ing away for dear life. *Sometimes*, I think to myself, *my life is boring.*
I look up from my pillow and stare at the clock. It's nine 'o'clock, so
I probably should get ready for bed.

Once again, I get up and stumble to the bathroom, where I close the door and grab the toothbrush that was floating in the air above the charging platform. After I brush my teeth, I peel off my clothes and turn on the water in the bathtub and stand in the hot water of the shower until all of the steaming hot water runs out.

When I get out of the shower, I put on my bunny pajamas, comb my hair, slip on the cat slippers and plop downstairs to the kitchen. Mascao stands at the counter in the dark, looking down at his hands. I switch on the light and carefully tiptoe over to Mascao.

"Hey," I tell him, "What's wrong?" I tap his shoulder, but it seems like he didn't even feel it at all.

"Fired," I hear him mumble. I gasp a little and he turns to look at me.

"April," he says, "the truth is, I was fired. Because…" He pauses for a moment and scratches the back of his head. "Cody didn't break into the military Training Center. And you already told me that. I believe you. But…" Mascao pauses again to glance at me. "The Head of the military found out, and… And he accused me of coming up with a false alarm, even though I didn't do this. He fired me and… I'm supposed to be Executed." Mascao gives me a sad smile.

This isn't real. My older brother, the one who cherished and protected and loved me for my entire life since our parents died, is going to be Executed. *Executed.* The word swirls through my mind again and again until it doesn't sound like a word anymore.

But then I realize it: Cody was the one who set up this false alarm, so the soldiers could hear the alarm from the Training Center, and he could do this own thing. Suddenly rage swells up inside me so hot that I don't feel like crying anymore. I want to kill him. He's the reason Mascao's going to be Executed. Him. Cody. *Cody.*

But I remember what he said to me earlier today. *I notice very little people, April, and you're among 1% of the Government that I notice.*

Different emotions flutter through me. Confusion, sadness, rage, concern, suspicion.

Mascao looks at me thoughtfully as my mind pounds with thoughts. I feel so overwhelmed that I walk away from Mascao and flump onto the couch.

I still don't understand.

CHAPTER 14

A s I fly through the streets of the Poor Sector, I think about what the Elector is doing, and what is going on in the Government. I pass a flyer on a building that says, "WANTED: Red-head disguised as news reporter for knowing too much Information. REWARD." I duck behind a building and take off the cap, setting it on the ground before ripping off the wig. I place the cap back on my head and decide to keep the colored contacts so no one would recognize me.

After I change into clean (stolen) clothes, I walk back out from behind the building. I stroll about the streets until I see it: My house.

I stumble to the backyard and crawl under our back porch. Everything is pitch-black, and it feels like I can almost hear insects and spiders crawling around me and I shiver at the thought. A light flickers through the basement window, and I peer inside. Wringing out dirty water from a dark gray shirt, 13-year-old Jade glances over her shoulder to check 5-year-old Crystal's progress on dunking dirty laundry into another bowl full of dirty water and scrubbing it clean. I scan the tiny basement once more until I'm sure that no one else is there. I quietly tap on the window and Jade and Crystal almost immediately notice me. They both get up and suspiciously walk over to the window, Jade sliding it open.

"Cody?" she asks. "Is that you?" She and Crystal squint at me and I realize that I still have my colored contacts on.

"Yeah," I whisper, "I have colored contacts on, 'cause, ya know…" I reach one hand to one of my eyes and the girls nod. I stretch into a more comfortable position on the ground under the porch as I tell them what happened. Disguising myself as a red-head news reporter to find out more about me and the Government, meeting Ty, him telling me about the Elector President capturing and Executing innocent people that have suspicions about him, the Senate, or the Government, how he got arrested for telling too much Information, and how I got arrested for knowing too much Information. Since Crystal has an eidetic memory, she already memorized the story by heart by the time I'm finished, and could announce how many times I said "uh". Jade's shaking her head, and I know that this means how disappointed she is in me.

"Ya know, if ya didn't just 'go with the flow' we wouldn't be here having this conversation," Jade remarks annoyingly, crossing her arms. I sigh at her and turn to face Crystal, who has a concerned look on her face.

"Cody," she says with a touch of worry in her tone, "Do you know what you have to do?" I shake my head at her.

"You're going to have to break into the Government Building, and destroy the Generator."

Soon Crystal's flipping through huge books trying to look for the definition of "Generator". I peer at the title of the huge book she's skimming through. "The History of the Government," Crystal mumbles to me as if she's reading my mind. She really knows me.

"Ah, here we are," she pipes up all of a sudden that makes Jade and I perk up. "Ahem. 'The Generator, a massive structure built in the heart of our very own Elector President's office, is hidden so cleverly that no one else know where it is except for our glorious leader himself. The Generator powers all of the Government, inside and out.'" Crystal pauses and flips through a couple more pages in the book. "'The Disparate are the different. In the Government, Trials are taken every year for pupils to test their IQ, strength, swiftness, and cleverness. The Correspondent are the normal. They finish their Trial with a Result that pleases everyone, and they get a degree, and a good college. The Disparate finish their Trial with a Result that leaves the Senate and the Elector President in confusion. They are still accepted to go to school, but soon, they vanish. No one knows of them, and where they went. Executioners at the Execution Center refuse to speak of this, and so does the Senate with the Elector.'"

I raise my eyebrows in worry. This means, that I have to destroy the Government's weakness, the Generator.

CHAPTER 15

E ventually I fall into a deep sleep on the couch and Mascao drapes a soft blanket over me.

I dream that I'm back outside near the Wall, where I first tasted the apple. Rocky's not with me, and I don't hear the whistling of the wind, or the chirping of the birds. I blink and suddenly I'm on the other side of the Wall, where pointy boulders stick out of the ground, and the rubble of a burned down house is scattered all over the place. I look to my left and press a hand against the Wall. It feels cold, and real. Mascao appears on the other side, pressing his hand on the glass with mine. His eyes are filled with tears, and his cheeks are hollow. His mouth starts to move, but I can't hear anything.

"Mascao!" I shout to him. "What are you saying? What's wrong?!" I stare at him through the glass Wall with horror and watch as he dissolves into thin air. I pound on the glass ferociously until I make a little crack and stop to look at it. Then I resume and continue to punch the glass until it shatters. Through the falling glass, I can just make out the Elector President, walking towards me, with a saw in his hand.

I jerk awake, throwing off the blanket to find myself still in the dark. I glance at the glowing clock implanted onto the wall. It's 3:49. I should at least sleep.

I grope around on the floor until I find the blanket and cover myself with it, plopping back down onto the couch. What was the Elector doing in my dream? Clutching my head in anticipation, I stand back up and quietly clap once to turn on a dim light. I walk over to the bookshelf that stands next to the television and run my hand across the book until I find the book that I want: The History of the Government. I already learned some of this stuff in school, but I'm pretty sure we didn't learn all of it. I sit on the couch and flip through the book. A chapter makes me stop skimming through the giant book, and I peer at it curiously. *The Disparate and the Correspondent*, it says.

It's going to be a long night.

CHAPTER 16

⟨⎯⎯⟩

T he next morning, I awake under the porch and immediately panic until I realize that I'm at my house. I breathe a sigh of relief and turn over to face the window to find Jade and Crystal gone. They're probably upstairs in their room.

I shift onto my stomach and wiggle out from the porch into daylight, squinting until my eyes get used to the brightness. The Poor Sector is surprisingly quiet today, and I slip the cap back onto my head with suspicion. As I stroll along the streets, I take note of the eerie silence that wavers around me. There's no one squeezed in between dark alleys or shouting out advertisements. For a second I panic when I consider me being deaf, and check my hearing by snapping my fingers in front of each ear. My suspicion is growing, and just in case, I slide into a dark alley and pull the cap lower over my face. I come across the dead end and examine the cracks and crevices in the brick wall. Many of them are big enough for me to shove a foot into each one, so I place one foot in the first crack, and begin to climb with my sack thumping against my side. I find myself on a roof of a building that looks to be about six stories tall, and I stagger to the edge to scan the Poor Sector. It's completely empty. Suspicion is replaced with panic in me as I get up and jump to the next building. It's even taller than the first one, so it'll give me a better view. I stand at the edge of the building and find the Versa Sector from the view. A JumboTron is sticking out of the horizon and it's flashing a signal I can just barely make out.

Take Cover

Panic is bubbling up inside of me when I realize that it must be a drill. If it's real, then there would be bombs dropping out from the sky, and there would be more noise. I begin to calm down while reassuring myself that it's next to impossible to break through the Wall. I once read in school that the Wall is made of a special indestructible glass, and at the very top, there is a sensor that could tell if we are under attack, and it would release an invisible force field that would protect our city. Even though I'm the Government's most wanted Criminal, I know that I have to do the Drill, just in case it actually was real.

I hop back down into the alley and crouch down, screwing up myself into a ball. I wait for the announcements to go off that the Drill is over and we could "continue with our every-day activities and/or errands". Counting the seconds in my head, I think about what would happen if we really *were* under attack. The city would be in ruins. Flames would leaps out at every corner. Woman would be running about the streets with their children. Soldier would march up and down the blocks with their weapons raised. Everything would be total chaos, not silent. I raise my head when I count up to minute ten. The Drill should be over by now. Maybe the Elector is doing something in his office, with the Generator or something. Maybe *he's* the one planning the attack. I'm just about to get up to alert Jade and Crystal back home when the announcements finally go off.

"Thank you for cooperating. This was just a drill. You may now continue with your every-day activities and/or errands. Have a nice day." I get up and straighten my shirt before strolling back out of the alley with my hat tipped even lower over my eyes. When I exit the alley and emerge into the sunlight, people are already pouring out of their homes and mumbling to each other. I don't know where I should go now. April hates me, and my family can't help me, because I could put them into danger.

And then it hits me: I could break Ty out of prison.

CHAPTER 17

This week is Trial week at school.

The Trial is a test that goes on at our school for the entire week near the end of the school year to test our swiftness, cleverness, reflexes, and wits. The Trial Board assigns each of us classes depending on how well we did on the PreTrial that we just took two days ago. I'm pretty sure I did average on it, so I might be assigned five or six classes. The most classes I've ever seen someone have for the Trial was eight classes.

I only have one day to prepare my belongings for the Trial. During the Trial, the students have to stay in dorms at the school. I'm going to have to be prepared.

After the Drill, I run up to my room and pull out a plain bag from my closet and place it on my bed. I reach underneath the levitating bed and pull out a normal shoebox. Inside the shoebox contains a pocketknife with some other tools that I could pull out, a large coil of wire, and a flashlight. I carefully place the objects in the bag and turn back around to find some clothes for the Trial.

Soon I have my bag packed with some hair elastics, a comb, some socks, two pairs of black waterproof leggings, a pair of gloves, two t-shirts, some underwear, a water bottle filled with water, a water purifier, a notebook, some pens and pencils, and a really old type of reading material called a book about the plants and wildlife of the world. I also change into another pair of purple waterproof leggings, a plain gray t-shirt, a jacket that used to be Mascao's, and some socks with my boots pulled over them. Even though it's almost summer in the Government, it can be cold. Finally, just in case, I stick a bobby pin in my hair and tie my hair up into a high ponytail.

I find Mascao downstairs watching TV while Oreo hops around on the rug. Mascao beams when I come to him and motions for me to sit down in between him and Whiskers.

"I can't believe it's your final year at school, and you're going to the Trial!" Mascao exclaims, pulling me close to him. I smile at him and scratch the head of an eager Whiskers.

"Can you tell me about *your* Trial?" I ask Mascao. He frowns.

"Well, I don't really remember much of it," he begins, "But I do have a warning for you: Always have your bag packed. Don't unpack it. Also, memorize names and faces if there are new people there. You're gonna have to determine whether they're your friend or your enemy. And, don't show people your weaknesses. They're gonna try to manipulate you so they could win. *Trust no one*, April. Even Rocky." The sound of Rocky's name makes my heart drop down into my stomach. "Also, always be prepared. You never know when they're gonna throw a round of the Trial at you." Suddenly Mascao gives me a look so sincere and serious that it makes me worry.

"But," I start to protest, "will you be here when I come back?"

Mascao smiles sadly at me. "The day of the Execution will be in two weeks. So yes, I will still be here when you come back." I breathe a sigh of relief and give him a hug.

When we arrive at the school, there's a crowd of students already piled in front of the building. Mascao and I exit the aircar and he brings my head to his chest one more time, kissing the top of my head.

"You'll do great on the Trial," he assures me. "Remember, this is the most important Trial of all and will greatly affect your life if you fail." I feel my stomach churn when Mascao says the word "fail".

"Promise me you'll be here when I come back," I murmur and shift the bag into a more comfortable position on my shoulder.

"I promise," Mascao tells me and pats my shoulder before stepping back into the aircar.

"Welcome to the yearly Trial!" the voice of Professor Hestridge, the head of the school, booms and everyone immediately goes silent. "There has been some changes this year." The second after Professor Hestridge says that, all the students burst into murmuring and exclamations.

"This year, instead of one week of the Trial, we will have two weeks." My mouth drops open. I can't stay here for two weeks. Mascao would be dead by the time I return. I fight the lump that's rising up in my throat as Professor Hestridge continues. "Since the amount of time you will be staying here has been extended, more rounds to the Trial will be added. Instead of five Trial rounds, you will be having eight Trial rounds, all that will be testing you on your swiftness, reflexes, cleverness, wits, and agility. Now I will hand the podium to our special guest, Gunner Valdez, a long-known coach for the Trial. Here we go!" Professor Hestridge brings up his arm as everyone applaudes hesitantly. Gunner, a beefy soldier with a scar streaked across his eye and his curly hair dyed purple, trots onto the stage and takes place before the podium. He waits for the applause to die down before he begins talking.

"I have some advice for ya'll: Don't die. Stay alive. Even though these Trials aren't made for ya'll to die, someone could be stupid enough to get himself in trouble, and he could *die*." All of the students gasp in return as Gunner continues talking.

"This year, we'll be throwin' *more* dangerous and brutal stuff than last year, and the year before that, because this is your last year at this school, so we're gonna determine whether you're *Disparate* or *Correspondent*. The Disparate *die*. An' the Correspondent finish the Trial with a good Result that gets them in a good college and they get a good life. So try to get a good Result so you could get in a college afterwards. Also be careful so you don't die. That's all I have to say. Thank you." Gunner steps off of the stage and Professor Hestridge takes his place behind the podium.

"All right! Now, I will be calling names in alphabetical order so the student can pick up his or her bracelet. You will have to keep these on at all times, and there will be a specific symbol on it that will represent you. Your symbol will also be on your door to your room,

so you might not want to lose these bracelets. Okay, so here we go…
Allaben, Hannah…"

I tune out for a moment because I don't feel like listening to all
the names being called. My last name is Ingalls, so there will be a
little time in between until Professor Hestridge calls my name.

"Dale, Rochelle."

I perk up when I hear Rocky's name being called and watch her
as she steps up onto the stage and Professor Hestridge slips a silver
bracelet onto her wrist and clicks it shut. Rocky proudly swishes off
of the stage to join the group of students standing behind the stage
before the entrance of the school. She's wearing a camouflage jacket
with a black t-shirt underneath with gray leggings and some old
worn-out boots. I nervously wait with my foot tapping the asphalt
until Professor Hestridge gets to the "I" section.

"Ingalls, April."

With all eyes towards me, I hop onto the stage and stand before
Professor Hestridge. I roll up my sleeve of my jacket and bring my
arm up. He snaps on a gleaming silver bracelet on my wrist with an
infinity symbol. I push my sleeve back down and step off of the stage
to join the crowd. Rocky stands at the bottom step of the set of stairs
in front of the entrance, waving me over and I happily walk to her
and whisper, "What kind of symbol did you get?"

Rocky grins at me and unveils her bracelet underneath her sleeve.
Her symbol is a scale with a star inside of it. I give her a thumbs up
and her smile grows so wide that I'm afraid the edges of her lips are
going to rip open.

We stand together, holding hands the rest of the time.

CHAPTER 18

I find myself at the edge of the Poor Sector, scouring the streets and buildings for the jail. Since Ty knows so much about what the Elector President could be planning to do to the Government, I could break him out of prison and tell him everything and ask him for help.

It's the middle of the day, so I need to be careful no one would see me. I squeeze myself in the backs of buildings and in dark alleys so no one would spot the Government's most notorious criminal lurking the grounds of a poor and innocent place. The Jailing Center is standing right across the street, and I think it's safe for me to cross without getting caught since I still have the colored contacts on to cover my freakishly bright blue eyes. I step out from in between two buildings and look around to see if there are any soldiers. The only soldiers that are on the block are the little kids who run around pretending that they're soldiers. I casually stroll across the street and enter the Jailing Center. Inside, the only light source is a dim light that's illuminating the ceiling, and everything is painted black. There are no windows at all, and I can barely see a thing. A black desk stands on the far left side with a young man sitting behind it. His feet are propped up on the desk and he lounges back on his chair (that is also black) with a TouchPad that he holds in front of his face. I approach him and start to talk.

"Um, excuse me," I say hesitantly. "I came to see someone."

The man brings the TouchPad from his face, and for the first time I can see him. He has curly black hair, braces poking out from in between his lips, and light brown eyes that I could just make out from underneath the dim light.

"Yeah?" he man responds, clearly annoyed.

"Tyler Black?" I shrug.

"Oh, um. Lemme see here..." The man taps a couple of things on the TouchPad as he brings his legs off of the desk. "Wait, sorry there, bro. There is no 'Tyler Black' here at this jail."

My heart starts to pound. No Ty? That would only mean one thing...

Tyler Raven Black is going to be Executed.

CHAPTER 19

W e all stand in the school's Assembly Room just after everyone's been assigned a bracelet. Professor Hestridge stands again on the stage with Gunner and a group of older students standing near him.

"And now we stand here in the Assembly Room, where we are going to assign a group of students to a mentor. Your mentor will assist you with homework, studies, anything. Again, we are going to assign them to you alphabetically. We will once more begin with Allaben, Hannah. You will be assigned to Tessa. Come on up."

I watch as Hannah, with her strawberry-blonde hair tied up in a ponytail whipping behind her, steps onto the stage and joins a woman who looks to be about twenty-years old with a nose piercing and her jet-black hair pulled up in a tight bun. It will be a while until Professor Hestridge gets to my name again. I wait with my hands behind my back and my feet rocking back and forth as I watch people being assigned to their mentors.

"Ingalls, April."

I perk up when I hear my name being called, and I cautiously step onto a stage with Professor Hestridge's hands up towards a young man that looks to be about Mascao's age. His hair is a curly blonde—only men ages 30 and older need to have comb-overs—and he has blue eyes that look faded into a gray color, and he flashes a smile at me. "You will be assigned to Grey," Professor Hestridge tells me, and I nod, joining Grey's side.

All of us are piled in a cozy-looking room with a fireplace and the lights died down, boys on one side and girls on the other side, with the mentors up front. I watch as Grey steps out of the group of mentors and faces all of us.

"You will now be assigned to your rooms," Grey shouts out, even though all of us are silent. "The boys are on the second floor, and the girls are on the third floor. You will not be assigned to roommates. To find your room, look for your symbol. You will find it on your bracelet. This will be your room for studies, sleeping, bathing, and relaxing. This room is the Lounge. All of you can come here to talk with your friends or just sit back and relax. The Dining Hall is to your right. The lights are on when it's open, but when it's closed, you're gonna have to make your own lunch in the Food Bar, which is next to the entrance. You have three days to settle down and make yourselves at home. All right, now boys, follow me upstairs, and girls, wait for the boys to find their rooms, and then you guys can go on."

There is commotion for a while as all the boys march after Grey upstairs while us girls stand deadly quiet, waiting for the chaos to die down. Tessa stands up front with her arms crossed and an expression I can't quite tell while all of us stare at her curiously.

"Okay," Tessa says, glaring at all of us, shifting her arms to her hips. The rumbling of the boys stomping the floor on the level above us dies down and Tessa walks over to the foot of the stairs, waving us over. We follow her as she starts climbing the stairs, and we do the same.

Soon we're all settled on the third floor and we press against the wall of the hall, waiting for Tessa to say something else.

"All right," Tessa begins, clapping her hands together. "You know what to do. To find your room, look for your symbol. That's gonna be easy 'cause you have the symbol already on your bracelets." When Tessa says the word "bracelets", everyone immediately glances down at their gleaming bracelets to make sure they know their symbols. Just like the others, I pull back my sleeve to make sure I know my symbol. The infinity symbol is still there, and I trace my pointer finger across the entwined silver.

"Okay, then," Tessa continues, "You can start looking for your rooms. Remember that we have a feast in the Lounge at six. Don't be late, or you won't be able to have a seat."

As soon as Tessa says that, all of the girls start bustling around while I stand, waiting for the commotion to die down. It's better to find my room later than to shove people around, trying to squeeze in between them. I spot Rocky upon the crowd the same time as she spots me, and she runs over to me.

"It's better to wait for this chaos to die down," she tells me, and I nod in agreement.

"You're right," I respond to her.

Rocky and I walk next to each other as we stroll along the long hallway. Suddenly Rocky shouts out and I jump, startled.

"There's my room," she exclaims, pointing to a door with a symbol of a scale with a star inside of it. I give her a thumbs-up as she enters her room, and when she disappears, I give a sigh of exasperation. I still haven't found my room. And I may be the last one to find it.

Just as I'm about to give up and go downstairs to the Lounge to wait for everyone else, I come across a door with my symbol: the infinity symbol.

I assume it's good luck, and head inside.

The room is bigger than the living room and the kitchen at my house; a queen-sized bed with an ordinary quilt and pillows stands against the wall, and there is a door to the balcony outside with an astounding view: the orchard where Rocky last took me near the Wall.

Light floods inside the room, which makes it easy to see. On the right side of the room is the bathroom, and a television is implanted on the left of the doorway.

I walk over to the bed and hop onto it, shifting myself to a cross-legged position, and I begin to unpack most of the things I don't need that much: the pens and pencils, the notebook, and the book. I let myself be aware of Mascao's warning to always be prepared.

Just as I'm about to leave the room with my bag, everything suddenly goes pitch-black, I feel the lock on the other side of the doorknob click, and the first round of the Trial begins.

CHAPTER 20

N ow I have to come up with *another* disguise in order for me to get inside the Execution Center.

And I know exactly what.

I swing along ledges of windows, run across the roofs of buildings, and crawl through and in between dark alleys to get to the store that I always "visit": the Party Store.

I peek inside the store to find the guy I want. Jeff. He stands behind the counter polishing something or other. Jeff is the manager of the Party Store, (not that anyone holds parties anymore) and he knows me as Cris. I glance at my reflection on the window to make sure I still have the colored contacts, and sure enough, they're still there, clearly covering my bright blue eyes. I pull my cap even lower over my eyes and open the door, walking inside.

Jeff immediately spots me and drops the things he was holding in his hands. His eyes light up with recognition as he approaches me.

"Cris!" he exclaims. "How you doin'!" Jeff gives me a big bear hug and I tense up a little, but not so much that he'll notice.

"Hey," I greet him and step back from his arms. "I'd like to have a wig."

"*Again?*" Jeff pipes up. "What do you use the wigs for, anyway?"

Dang. Now I need to search for a lie. I hesitate for a moment before I reply, "Ya know, for pranking my family and such."

Jeff guffaws with laughter and I can't help but smile a little.

"Okay, which one?" Jeff steps back and brings up his arm to show the wide selection of wigs hanging on the wall. There's blonde wigs, red wigs, brown wigs, even rainbow wigs!

"Um…" I put my hand onto my chin and observe the selection of wigs. I could take the brown wig and put fake tan on me and pretend to be a sobbing relative of Tyler's. That could do.

"I'll take this one," I say to Jeff, pointing at a normal boys' brown wig.

"'Kay." Jeff grabs a stool that was leaning against the counter and places it below the wig section. He steps onto the stool and grabs the wig that I wanted for the disguise. When Jeff gets off, he hands me the wig and tells me, "All right, that'll be one hundred Books."

That's pretty cheap. For me, that is. I reach into my bag and pull out a jumble of Books out and give it to Jeff.

"Thanks," I say and tuck the wig into my bag.

"No, sir, thank *you*." Jeff smiles at me and I wave goodbye before exiting the store.

I hide in another dark alley where no one would see me, and pull out the wig. I change into new clothes and take out the hair mask, stretching it onto my head and tucking in any loose hair. It looks like it's getting late, which means that Ty has just a couple more hours left to live. With the wig placed carefully on my head, I step out from the alley and start to cross the street, where the Execution Center sits.

The lobby looks empty except for the woman typing away on the computer at her desk. I swing open the door and the second I walk inside, I sniffle and pretend to sob. That makes the woman notice.

"What's wrong, dear?" The woman looks up from the computer and puts on a concerned look on her face.

"My dad…" I pause for a moment before wailing again, "He's gonna be *Executed*!"

"Well, I can set you an appointment with your father, is that alright, dear?" the woman asks me. I nod in response. "Now, who's your father?"

I reply as quickly as I can, but not that quick so the woman won't get suspicious. "Tyler Black."

The woman nods in understanding and turns her attention back to the computer before typing a few words. I shift the bag full of weapons and clothes on my shoulder and blink up at the woman.

"Mmm hmm," the woman says and turns to face me. "Yes, your father is still here. You can go visit him one last time, dear."

"THANK YOU SO MUCH!" I exclaim with fake delight and beam at the woman. She smiles at me and gestures toward the airchairs lined up near the window. I gratefully obey and order myself another cup of coffee from the armrest delivery. As I sip the coffee, I glance at my watch to check the time. It's almost seven. Tyler has little time left to live.

I wait some more until the woman finally speaks up, "Um, I'm sorry, dear. Your father is already dead."

CHAPTER 21

I jiggle the doorknob to find out that it's no use; it's locked. This should be a test for our wits. I shuffle through my bag until I find what I need: the flashlight. I knew I would need it. I click it on and examine the door and the lock. This should be pretty easy.

When I was little, I used to get into trouble all the time at home, and Mascao would lock me in my room. I always had bobby pins with me, and after ten minutes I always would come strolling out of my room triumphantly.

This lock looks to be about the same as the lock I have in my room. But I don't have the right tool to pick through it. I stick the flashlight in between my knees and scour through my bag to find the pocket knife-tool thing. After some flipping through the different kinds of tools I have in the tool thing, I remember that I put a bobby pin in my hair before leaving. I feel through my hair and pull it out before securing it in the keyhole. I wiggle the bobby pin around in the small hole and feel a click. Excitement bubbles up inside of me as I carefully turn the doorknob and burst through the door. I can't help but smile at myself and turn off the flashlight, placing it back into my bag. With the bobby pin back in my hair, I proudly trot downstairs into the Lounge, where Gray and a bunch of other mentors are sitting around the fireplace and chatting. They immediately stopped talking when they notice me, and suddenly they stand up and start to applaud.

"First Breaker!" someone shouts and Gray walks up to me.

"What's going on?" I ask him, confused.

"You are the first person to complete the first round of the Trial," Gray explains. "It took you…" He glances at his watch. "I donno, two minutes?"

"*Two minutes*?!" I breath. I can't believe I could be *that* fast to break out of a room.

"Yup." Gray waves his arm towards the seats that are lined up around the fire. "Have a seat. Relax. There's still ten more minutes until the feast begins. The people who are late have to clean up after us."

"Okay." I take a seat in a comfy-looking chair that sits off to the side. As I wait, Gray and the other mentors chatter and laugh as they stand huddle on a large couch.

I haven't been waiting for another two minutes when another boy with chestnut-brown hair bursts downstairs with sweat glistening on his forehead and dripping all over the rug. It seems that he broke out of his room using strength. The mentors applaud again.

"Second Breaker!" someone else shouts. The boy looks perplexed, and he looks over to me. Suddenly anger flashes across his eyes and he gives me such an intimidating look that I know I have to be careful with who I trust. Mascao was right.

I need to determine who's my friend or my enemy.

CHAPTER 22

N ow I don't know what to do.

How could Ty be *dead* already?

Maybe I should trick April into helping me. I still have my disguise on, so all I have to do is be "Cris", and she'll fall for it. But first, I have to find April.

The Versa Sector is just a couple blocks away, so it won't take me that much time to find her, I guess.

As I run across the roofs of buildings, I strain to remember what she looks like, even though I just met her yesterday. I just had so much on my mind, I barely remember anything. During the last three years of my life, the only thing I've been thinking about was plotting my attack against the Elector President. I'm *still* plotting my attack, and I'm trying to remember faces of friends and enemies at the same time.

So, April has silky brown hair, olive-green eyes, braces, and she looks small for her age.

I try to squeeze the information into my head next to my plotting of my attack. Brown hair. Green eyes. Braces. Short.

Just as I finish going over the information I keep in my head about April, I get to the outskirts of the Poor Sector. The Versa Sector is stretched out below me as I stare at the aircars passing by. In the Poor Sector, there are very little aircars because people can barely afford to buy them.

The sun seems to be just above the horizon, so that means I have little time. I race across the rooftops of building until I can just make out the sign that sticks out of the ground below me:

Welcome to the Versa Sector

I decide I can stop trying to hide myself, because, judging by the looks of me, it doesn't look like I just came out from underneath a porch in the Poor Sector.

Immediately the scenery changes as I cross the line that divides the Versa Sector with the Poor Sector. Identical brick houses stand side by side, more aircars zoom by, and the road looks freshly paved. (Not that the aircars need the road.)

There are JumboTrons pointed high up in the sky displaying news. I watch from the sidewalk as one JumboTron flashes some news that changes everything I have planned:

"VERSA STATE HIGH SCHOOL BEGINS TRIAL WEEK."

CHAPTER 23

⟨⎯⎯⎯⟩

I patiently wait for the other students to come downstairs when suddenly one of the mentors shouts, "Mealtime!" Butchers with white aprons tied on their waists stroll into the Lounge and place plates of lamb chops, mashed potatoes, dessert... EVERYTHING.

All the other students (only three more came after the "Second" Breaker) dig into the feast while I stay where I am, uncertain to make my choice. I glance up to Gray, who winks at me and whispers, "Go on. Eat." Then I smile, lean over, and help myself to a salad, mashed potatoes, and the lamb chops. As I eat my dinner, I glance over to the other four first Breakers eating hastily like a pack of wolves. The mentors are grouped up in front of the fireplace, chatting and laughing.

How are they not hot? I wonder to myself. *It's like a sauna in here.*

I clear my plate pretty quickly and help myself to seconds. The food is so good, how can you reject these solid objects cooked from heaven and sent down here by the messenger angel, Gabriel? I sure wish I was hungrier. By the time I'm done, the mentors stand in front of us, trying to make eye contact. Are they intimidating us? If they are, it sure is working. I place my plate on the table and squirm uncomfortably in my seat.

"Well, then," Gray says. "Since this place looks like a pigsty, it'll be perfect for the Lasters to clean up. It's sorta like a punishment for them."

Last-ers. Does Gray mean the last Breakers?

81

A girl raises her hand. "Why do they get a punishment?"

"Ah," Gray replies. "That is because we will only pick out the top five people in each Trial round. And then we count up the points with Hestridge."

"So we're the top five?"

"Exactly."

"Who's the first one?"

"Why, it's this lovely lady name April Ingalls." Gray nods his head towards me and I feel my face getting warm as the girl gives me a nasty look. Meanwhile, Gray casually reaches into his pocket and pulls out the last thing I would expect him to pull out–a pack of cigarettes.

"Seriously?" I ask him as he lights up the butt of his cigarette.

"What?" Gray slips the match back into his pocket. The cigarette dances in his mouth as he speaks.

"This is the last thing I expect you to do. The *last thing*." I raise an eyebrow at him as he pulls out the cigarette and makes an O, attempting to make smoke rings, but failing.

"The last thing?" Gray smirks at me as I blush profusely and sink lower into the couch, hoping the cushions would swallow me up.

I've been sitting for the past ten minutes, thinking about everything until I couldn't take it. I politely ask myself to be excused and head upstairs, scanning the doors for my symbol.

The moment I spot the one door that is out in the very back of the hall with the infinity symbol, I enter it and softly close the door behind me. There are still banging and shrieks of girls screaming for help and helplessly trying to get out of their rooms by banging and kicking their doors.

I clap twice to turn on the lights and spot a flashing towards my direction. A key sits on the one desk that is off to the side next to the entrance to the bathroom. I immediately grab it and tuck it away into my bag, where it would be safe. The sun is setting on the horizon, and the view looks beautiful. I've never seen anything beautiful before, because in the city apparently the Elector President doesn't want anyone else attracted to someone or something else that isn't him.

One glance at the dark bathroom and I decide I should take a shower to freshen up. With my bag left on my bed, I make sure the door to my room is locked and take off my clothes, turning on the water in the faucet. I stand in the shower and scrub everything on my body as if it would wash away my problems.

Even though it's nine when I get out of the shower, I go to bed anyway. I brush my teeth thoroughly and leave the toothbrush and toothpaste near the sink. Since I never thought of packing any pajamas, I go to sleep in the purple leggings, a pair of socks and a gray shirt.

* * *

Instead of a pleasant dream, I drift off into sleep getting a nightmare. But this time I'm not at the orchard. I'm in an office. There's a bookshelf behind a desk with papers piled on it. I hear rumbling and moaning, as if there was a thunderstorm going on outside. Unfortunately, there are no windows for me to peek out.

Suddenly I hear a door open, and look to my right to see a soldier enter the room.

"Sir?" he says.

"Um, I'm not a sir," I reply, irritated.

"But sir, you are our glorious Elector President, of course you must be adored and glorified." The response hits me so hard I also fall over. Apparently, in this dream, I'm the President.

"Okay," I simply say.

The soldier clears his throat. "We have loaded the guns with the sleeping serum, sir. Why don't you make sure the Generator is in full power?"

"Uh, all right…" I turn to my desk, perplexed and looked back at the soldier. "Where exactly is the 'Generator'?"

The soldier stares back at me with wide eyes. "But sir, aren't you the only one who knows where the Generator is?"

This doesn't help at all. If he doesn't know where the "Generator" is and I don't know where the "Generator" is, then who knows where it is, and how can I make sure "it" is in full power?

"Can you at least tell me about the Generator?" I squeak to the soldier.

The soldier looks shocked. "Well, as you wish, sir. The Generator is a complicated piece of machinery, and is hidden so cleverly by, of course, you, that nobody else knows where it is. It powers the entire Government, inside and out. The invisible forcefield, the lights, the buildings, the businesses, *everything*. If it is destroyed, so is our beloved city.

"That is why the Generator is put in the hands of our most trusted leader ever–you, sir. You, as in the Elector President. Without you, our city would be in danger. You have a powerful job, sir. You take care of the Rules of the Government, you stop Crimes committed by Criminals like Cody Dalton Vares, and you keep the Generator safe.

"Most of all, you keep people from having any suspicions of your brilliant plan: for world domination. Remember your recent capture of Cody? Now he will think twice before nosing around in our business." It seems that the soldier is getting more and more comfortable about talking about the worst secrets of the Government.

"If you don't remember, sir, our plan is to poison the entire Government City with sleeping serum. Of course, you know that it lasts for twenty four hours. That will give us enough time to do our thing. While Government City is asleep, we go around the world and drug the entire population with sleeping serum so you can take over and have world domination. Unfortunately, the sleeping serum or sleeping pill doesn't work on the Disparate. So you know that we track the Disparate down by studying their Trial of brain scanning results and then Executing them afterwards. So I hope I answered all your questions, sir. You don't look well. Perhaps you hit your head and you now have amnesia? Oh, I'm sorry, sir. I hope you recover soon. I think maybe you should rest. All those hours going over the Rules of the Government must have exhausted you. Have a great night, sir."

And then the soldier left.

CHAPTER 24

I camp at the back of a store for the night where no one would see me. The next day I hope my clean clothes will fool people into thinking I'm part of the middle class. With my wig and colored contacts still on, I won't be recognized as the Government's most notorious Criminal casually strolling the grounds of Versa Sector.

My hope is that I'll find April, even though she is at school taking the Trial. Lately I've been having a strange connection with her, as if we're related or something. Or as if we're both *Disparate*. I can't believe I didn't think of that before!

As a stranger passes by me, I smile in greeting at him and he smiles back. I need to act normal so people won't get suspicious.

The goal is to get to Versa State High School without anyone drawing attention or anything.

In order to not get bored out of my mind as I walk, (the walk from the Poor Sector to the Versa State High School is long) I figure out what random objects are sdrawkcab. (for those who don't know, that means "backwards") Aircar, racria. School, loohcs. Government, tnemnrevoG. The possibilities are endless.

By the time I'm debating myself whether I could figure out thirty backward words, I'm already in front of the school.

Huh, I think to myself, *That went fast.*

But then the thought hits me: I have no idea where April is in that school.

I enter it anyway, and find a front desk where there was a woman (probably a secretary) reading a book instead of typing on a computer.

"Um, excuse me," I say to her and she immediately puts down the book on the desk. "I'd like to make an appointment."

"With whom?" the secretary asks me.

"April Ingalls?"

"All right," she responds. "You a relative?" I nod.

"Cris Ingalls."

"Full name?"

"Cristopher Noah Ingalls." It's the first name that popped into my head. The *first name*. But then I add, "But I like to be called Cris."

"Age?"

"21."

"Guardian?"

"I'm twenty one. I don't need a guardian."

"Relationship with April?"

"Cousin."

"Eye color?"

"Green."

"Hair color?"

"Isn't it kind of obvious? Brown." This lady's kind of getting specific.

"Height?"

"How should I know? I don't measure myself."

"Weight?"

"About one hundred eighty, I guess."

"Birth date?"

"The twenty second of August."

"Year?"

I do some of the quickest calculations in my head I have ever done in my life. "2013."

"Well." She smiles at me. "Looks like you survived the World War III. I'm assuming you were a military soldier."

"And I still am," I answer quickly. "That's why I travel a lot."

"With that little bag?"

"Yup. It's better to have less weight. I was heading towards Nalaska City in the underground train, but I decided to stop in the Government City and say hello to my cousins." The secretary chuckles, who knows why, and points towards a door to my right.

"In there's the Lounge. There are probably some older people who look to be about your age. They're mentors. Tell them you're visiting for April and one of them will lead you to her room."

"Thanks." I wave goodbye to her and push open the doors to the Lounge. I immediately notice a snack bar to my left and there are couches in front of me with a fireplace burning in front of them. There are some older people huddled around the fireplace, chatting and laughing.

I approach them.

"'Scuse me," I greet them. "I'm here to visit April Ingalls."

A guy with curly blonde hair in khaki shorts stands up from the group and faces me.

"I'll take you," he says. "Trials didn't start yet, and everyone's probably either at breakfast or in their rooms."

"'Kay," I reply. "Thanks."

I follow the guy upstairs until we make it to the third floor.

"Alright," the guy pipes up. "Just in case you need me, my name's Gray, just call Gray the Cool Guy whenever you're in trouble or whatever. April's room is at the way back. It has the infinity symbol on it. Just knock. If she doesn't answer, she's either sleepin' or she's in the dining room havin' breakfast or she's just havin' a bad temper and she won't let anybody in. Okay, my job is done. I'm gonna be in the Lounge. All the time. For a couple of hours. With my friends. If you need me. Bye now. See ya." And Gray left.

I don't want to be rude or anything, but this guy talks a lot. And he. Has. A lot. Of pauses. In his. Sentences.

When Gray leaves, I knock softly on April's door, and I hear some rustling when April opens the door.

"Uh...Who are you?" She asks me, confused.

"Cris, for now," I whisper and breeze past her into her room. Considering her expression, I guess visitors aren't welcome in April's room.

April closes the door and turns to face me.

"Seriously."

"I'm Cody," I tell her.

"Yeah, and I'm a unicorn from Rainbow Land," April responds sarcastically.

"Oh, that's because I'm in disguise." I give her a serious expression for her to believe me.

"Then...Whatcha wearin'?"

"Colored contacts, some clean clothes, and a wig."

"Prove it."

I really don't want to disgust her, so I politely excuse myself to go to the bathroom and carefully slip out the colored contacts. I blink a few times to keep my eyes from watering, and there they are. My old, freakishly polaroid blue eyes staring back at me through the mirror. Next I take off the wig and wig cap and reveal myself to April. She gasps.

"Holy crap," she exclaimed and brought her hands to her mouth. Not really the reaction I was expecting. I was expecting her a scream and barge out of her room. Maybe she's used to me or something.

"I really need to talk to you," I say, lowering my voice to a whisper just in case the walls aren't soundproof.

"About what?" April whispers back.

"Well, since I met you, I got this weird connection between you and me. I'm thinking it's because we're both Disparate or something."

April gasps again. "Oh my gosh, I was getting the same thing too! I guess I was Disparate my whole life, but the brain scannings we get every month don't work on me, and that's why I'm safe. No, wait!" She inhales sharply as I urgently wait for her response. "I get it now! I'm guessing the Government knew, but they were saving me for later or something. My brother got fired from the military, so I'm also guessing he didn't do anything wrong, his boss just found out he's Disparate! And I don't know why they're not Executing me yet."

"Maybe it's because of the Trials."

April snaps her fingers. "You're right. They can't just pull me out of the most important Trial of all. When I pass it, the Senate is going to go over my Results to make sure if I am Disparate and I'm worth Executing."

I shrug. "I don't think all the Disparate people are *born* Disparate. I think that at some point of their lives they realize how strange they're living and they begin to question the Rules of the Government and the Elector President and everything. I didn't have any suspicions about the Government at all until when I was twelve years old and they captured me, probably for being Disparate."

"Maybe you're right. I had a dream last night that probably solves *everything*. So I dreamed that I was the Elector President, and a soldier came inside and told me that all the gun were filled with sleeping serum. I had no idea what he was talking about, but I didn't question him. But then the soldier told me that I had to make sure the Generator was in full power for that. *That's* when I questioned him. Then, he told me everything.

"He told me that the Government's plan was to drug the entire Government City with sleeping serum so the Elector President can get out of there to take over the world by drugging the entire planet and then seizing control of the entire human population so he can have world domination.

"But then the soldier said that the sleeping serum doesn't work on the Disparate and that's why they get rid of them so no one would stop his plot."

This all makes sense. That's why the Government was capturing the Disparate! Another piece of the puzzle clicks into my mind as April continues.

"The soldier also told me about the Generator. He said that the Generator powers the entire Government. If it's destroyed, so is 'our beloved city'. So technically the soldier told me all of the Government's darkest secrets. My only question left is how all that information got into my dream somehow."

"I know about the Generator," I point out. "I read it once in a book. It said that the Generator is hidden in the Elector President's office so cleverly that no one else knows where it is. And if we want to get in there and destroy it, we have to travel one hundred stories, beat 500 soldiers, and find out where the Generator is in the first place."

"Well, when you say it, it sounds crazy and impossible." April smirks. "But the only thing that is impossible is impossibility."

CHAPTER 25

Now that Cody put all that crazy stuff into my head, I can't get rid of the thought. How can we get into the Government Building, and somehow get away with it?

I still hang on to that thought as I wait for Cody to put on his disguise and say goodbye to him and head downstairs into the Lounge to grab a snack from the Food Bar and when Gray (he seems to be the leader of the mentors) announces that we'll be getting our schedules and classes and when he started calling names to receive our schedules.

"Ingalls, April."

"Hmm?" I look up to see everyone staring at me and Gray holding a piece of paper in his hands.

"Come up to get your schedule."

"Um, okay." I hear a few snickering behind me as I step up to Gray to take the piece of paper. The snickering continues and I quickly head upstairs to my room. I'm guessing there won't be any important announcements, so it's probably okay to leave.

I set my bag on my bed and scan the sheet of paper. Nine classes. I have nine classes to keep up with for the next two weeks. And they could be adding more.

I read for a couple of hours until I hear some knocking on the door.

"Come in," I shout out, never leaving my bed. The doorknob turns and Rocky enters my room.

"'Sup," she greets me, plopping down on the bed next to me.

"Nothing much," I reply. "Just readin'."

"'Readin'?" Rocky asks me, her voice rising. "Not something cool like 'peelin'?"

"Nope."

"What's wrong?"

I sigh. "Do you think...Do you think you're suspicious about the Government?"

"What?" Rocky screeches. "No way. Government City is a clean place. The Elector President protects us and adds good rules to the Rules of the Government list."

Apparently Rocky's Correspondent. This is bad. This is really bad. I take out my hair from the ponytail and carefully weave it into a bun.

Rocky gasps. "Wait, don't tell me...You're Disparate? April, this is bad. You could get yourself killed!"

"Mascao's getting Executed. I think it's because he's Disparate too," I mumble.

"Gosh, April, how can you question the Elector President? He's like, the coolest guy ever! He keeps everyone safe from invaders and everything!"

"Rocky, you don't understand. The 'glorious' Elector is planning to drug the entire world with sleeping serum so he can take over the world!"

"That's good. Then he'll keep the entire world safe from danger. There'll be world peace."

"No, Rocky. Think of all the rules he'll add to the List. And there won't be any danger. Do you think aliens will invade us?"

"No, but..."

"God, Rocky! The Elector's bad! He's a dictator! He's trying to control us all!"

"Well, if you put it that way, it sounds terrible."

"That's because it is terrible! HE WANTS POWER OVER US ALL."

"He'll keep everyone safe!"

"No, he won't! Just get out of my room and don't come back until you change!"

"Fine." Rocky gets up and strolls over to the door. Before she leaves, she turns around. "Oh, right. I came to tell you that IQ tests start in an hour. Good luck." And then she leaves.

I harrumph a little and grab my bag, following Rocky at a safe distance downstairs into the Lounge.

The Lounge is already bustling with activity, and almost all the seats are taken, so I take one of the last seats left next to the "Second Breaker". He gives me a nasty look. I'm guessing that I'll be the most hated in the group.

This time instead of Gray, a guy with long brown hair up to his ears and brown eyes steps up in front of the group of mentors.

"Alright, ya'll," he yells and everyone immediately goes silent. "We're gonna be giving you your IQ tests. It's got about forty questions, but you gotta be wise. Your score is gonna be based on your accuracy and speed. Boys are gonna be takin' the test in one classroom, the girls will be takin' it in another classroom. So I'm goin' with the boys, and Tessa's goin' with the girls. Now this time it'll be ladies first." The guy brings his hands up to wave us away, and with Tessa leading, all of us pile out of the Lounge and down the hall into a large classroom. The classroom has white lights hanging from the ceiling, a pattern of an aqua blue and white in the tiles, a black chalkboard implanted on the wall in the front of the classroom, and the desks are organized by rows and columns. We all take a seat while Tessa waits up front for us to get settled. She passes out booklets of our IQ tests on our desks and says, "Don't open the tests until I tell you to."

We do as Tessa says and sit at our desks, blinking up at her nervously.

"Okay," she chortles. "The rules are to 1: don't cheat. 2: don't use any other information except for your brain. 3: This doesn't take really long, but take your time. The tests will be scored by *speed* and accuracy, remember, so maybe…don't take your time. Rush! You may begin."

It takes everyone a minute to realize that Tessa didn't give us any writing utensils because she wanted us to figure out on our own that we have to provide our own tools for everything. I quickly stick my hand in my bag and feel around for anything. A pen, a pencil, a marker, anything. I pull my hand out the moment I feel a stick-shaped object and find out that it's a pen. But it's good enough.

I flip open the cover and quickly scan the first question. *What is ½ of ¼ of ⅕ of 200?* This question is pretty easy. First I do ½ of 200, which is 100. Then I quickly calculate ¼ of 100, which is 25. Finally I do ⅕ of 25, which is 5, so 5 is my answer. I fill in the bubble next to the choice and move on to the next question.

It takes me about forty minutes to finish the IQ test, and I close the booklet of the test and pack up. I glance at Tessa, who is reading the *Daily Government*

newspaper, and figure that I can leave. With people still focused on their papers, I quietly slip out of the classroom and into the Lounge.

It seems that the mentors are always hanging out in there, because there they are, sitting near the fireplace. And talking. One of them turns around and spots me.

"Whoa, would you look at that. First IQ finisher," he says casually. The rest of the mentors turn around and stare at me. I feel my face turn red and ignore them, heading upstairs to my room.

I read the rest of the evening.

CHAPTER 26

The secretary let me sleep in a room that night. I rented it out with a lot of money, so of course it would absolutely (in British accent) *charm the little lady*!

I get out of bed and walk into the small bathroom, staring at the mirror, at my own reflection. The day of my interview with Ty swirls into my head. He had the same tattoo as my dad. A small black triangle. I examine my arms, my legs my back, and my collarbone to see if I have the same symbol of the small little triangle. A flash of something dark black comes out before my eyes and I check the same spot on my collarbone, and there's the triangle, looking as if it was fresh.

My discovery of the tattoo makes me question it. Did my parents give it to me when I was young? Does my entire family have it? Does April have it?

Maybe I should just ask her. I'll simply ask the secretary for another visit with April before I go on my way. I'm guessing I should return back home and ask Crystal and Jade if they have the symbol on their collarbones.

I hastily change from my dirty clothes into clean clothes, freshen up, and head downstairs to the lobby. The secretary is there, sitting at her desk, typing away on her computer, as usual. I breeze by her, thinking that I don't need to check in because the lady is just so (in British accent again) *charmed*!

It's empty in the Lounge, so I'm guessing it's early. I go to April's room anyway.

I knock on the door, and it takes a couple of seconds for her to answer it. She reveals herself, and she looks exhausted. Her hair is messed up, and her eyes look puffy and red with sleep.

"What?" she almost yells, irritated. Then her eyes go wide when she realizes who I am. "Get in here." April grabs my arm and pulls me into her room, slamming the door behind her.

"Well, since you're here now, we can sort of plan things out," she says, plopping down onto her bed.

I hesitate. "I have some questions for ya."

"Well, don't just stand there waiting for suspense, tell me!"

"Do you have the black triangle symbol on your collarbone?" I slightly pull my t-shirt out of the way to unveil my tattoo."

April stares at it for a moment until she gasps. "Oh my gosh!" She pulls at the hem of her shirt and I can make out the symbol of a black triangle.

"I think I know what this means," April pipes up, getting up and pacing back and forth across her room. "My brother has the tattoo too. Maybe this is the symbol for the Disparate!"

I kind of gasp softly in surprise. Does my entire family have the symbol too?

"We're gonna need to hide these from people," April continues, "They can arrest us or kill us or worse."

I want to ask, *What's worse than dying?* But then I answer myself, *Torture, probably.*

"So how do you think we can break into the Government Building?" I ask.

"We can disguise ourselves as soldiers," April answers almost immediately.

I gape at her. "How?"

"My brother's a soldier. Soon it'll be was." She cringed. "We can just go back to my house and get his uniforms. Then I can disguise myself as a boy, and you can disguise yourself as...Someone else."

That's a brilliant idea. If we keep our identity a secret, no one will know. But then a thought hits me.

"How will we get inside? We need an identification card to get into the most important building in the city."

April thought this through. "I can just disguise myself as Mascao and swipe his identification card from him, 'cause he probably won't need it anymore." She frowned for a few seconds, and suddenly lit up with a smile. "I know! We can break Mascao out from Execution and tell him our plan! He's Disparate, so he'll definitely help us." She beams at me, and I can't help but beam back at her. Again, this is a brilliant idea. April can dress up as a fake soldier, I can dress up as a fake soldier, and Mascao will have to disguise his looks.

"Wait...But then we can't use Mascao's identification card. People will know it's him and they'll arrest him and us all over again."

April groans. "Dang, you're right. I still want to help break Mascao out from Execution." She crosses her arms defensively. I sigh at her.

"Okay, fine. As long as he helps us." I cross my arms too and raise my eyebrows at her.

"I'm sure he will," April shoots back at me.

I wave my hands in the air to cut out our argument. "All right, all right, I know. But first we have to think about one thing and one thing only: How will we get inside the Building?"

April's face lights up after a few moments. "We can still disguise ourselves as soldiers, go to the Government Building's entrance, beat up the guys that are guarding the front entrance, swipe some of the identification cards, and bam! We're inside."

I nod in approval. "That's good. But second we need to think of a plan B. And we need to ask Mascao if he's in favor of this."

April nods back at me. "We can still disguise ourselves as soldiers, go up to the front entrance, and tell all the guys that it's their break time, and we can wait a few seconds in between telling each one."

"Well...Okay." I'm not so sure this will work. The guards might think that we're lying and they'll arrest us for sure. I'm just going to hope that plan A works and we won't have to do plan B in case it won't be a success.

"How about a plan C?" I ask.

"Well, what else is there?"

I was afraid she was going to ask that question. "One of us can distract the soldiers from someplace that is not too far, not too close away from the Building, and while they all rush over there or a few amount of guards stay there, we can either beat them up, or we can just go inside if the guards aren't there."

April nods, smiling. "Let's make that our plan A. Some guards are going to stay there to guard the entrance anyway. That'll be perfect for us to beat them up and grab their identification cards. Therefore, we're inside." Her smile grows as I look down shamefully on the ground. I hadn't thought this part through about the cards to get inside. But after, realizing that *I've* come up with a perfect plan A, and not April, I slowly grin from ear to ear.

"Sounds great," I say a little too happily.

"Okay," April finishes, seeming like she didn't hear me. "We're gonna have to escape the Trial somehow, break Mascao out from Execution, return back to my house, suit up, and get weapons. *Then* we go to the Government Building."

"You know, we aren't going to break your brother out from Execution that easily. The Senate banned invisible pills years ago."

April smirks. I have a feeling she's going to have a really stupid idea to get her brother out of Execution. "We pretend we're rebels."

"Oh crap," I almost shout.

"Just listen to me," April interrupts. "We pretend we're rebels. We destroy everything in the Execution Center, causing chaos. We find Mascao. We run out of there. We go back to my house before they realize who we are."

"Why don't we do something more peaceful," I cut in, "and disguise ourselves as Executioners?"

April considers this. "Or we could just sneak past that old lady who sits behind that stinkin' desk of hers."

"That could work. How about the distraction at the Building?"

"Well, there is the Military Center there where all the soldiers meet and chat and stuff like that. I can start a fire at the most unused room. That'll be a fuss for the soldiers while they try to find the room."

"And what's that room?"

"The old, abandoned, dirty, ugly, small, printer room."

I grin at April. This could work. The fire would set off the fire alarm, causing the soldiers to try and find the source. There will be a lot of soldiers in the Military Center.

And so we settle on a decision. We break Mascao out of Execution. We change into military outfits. We go for plan A at the Government Building. If that doesn't work, then plan B. If *that* doesn't work, then I don't know what else will work.

CHAPTER 27

After Cody leaves I immediately take a shower, put on some leggings, a plain t-shirt and my boots, brush my hair into a messy bun, and brush my teeth before heading downstairs.

Everyone's already in the Lounge, chatting and laughing with friends and snack on food from the Food Bar. All the seats are taken, and the Dining Hall is still open, so I head inside and grab myself a quick breakfast.

As I munch on toast, I think about what happened this morning. It went by so fast, it doesn't seem real at all. It just doesn't seem real that the Government's most notorious and wanted criminal and I are planning an attack against the city's most heavily guarded building, the Government Building.

I also think about Execution. Nobody knows what it's like, because nobody ever survives it to tell anyone. Only Cody knows, but the Executionists didn't even start the operation. Whenever I imagine what Execution is like, or at least try to, I imagine it a death serum, where the Executionists take you to the Operation Room and stick a needle in your arm, and then, bam, you're dead. No funeral, no chanting the person's name, no nothing. When you get Executed, there's no funeral set up. No people come to say their blessings. Mostly you get hatred. Once the news gets out that so-and-so committed a Crime and was Executed, people don't bless them and say that they probably lived a long, happy life and are now going to sleeping peacefully in Peacen ("Peacen" was once decided to be a landscape of peace for the dead). The people curse them, and spit towards their home or their family that they should go to Hell for raising such a stupid child.

After I finish my breakfast, I throw away my trash and go back into the Lounge, where the mentors are already gathered up at the front, with Gray leading them and his arms raised. The way his arms linger like that in the air reminds me of a hawk. Maybe he's trying to act like a hawk to show that he's watching all of us fail or succeed our Trial, the way hawks in real life watch all animals fail or succeed living.

"Settle down, everyone," he says, and everyone immediately goes silent. I can still hear people mumbling and whispering to each other. Everyone's probably anxious to hear what the next round is going to be. Gray puts his arms back down, and the image of the hawk printed in my brain vanishes.

"We're going to be starting the next round of the Trial," he continues. "A lot of you might not be happy. I've spoken with the Senate to set this up for you guys. So, here it is…" I feel everyone holding their breath. "You're going to be sent to Poverty."

Everyone immediately begins to react by shouting, crying, screaming, throwing tantrums, hugging, wailing. I just stand there with my eyes open wide and my heart in my throat. It *literally* feels like it's in my throat. I think I'm going to puke. I remember Gunner telling us the first day that the Trial rounds are *not* going to be deadly. Everybody lied to everybody. A terrible future is forming in my mind, where there's a civil war, everyone's suffering, and there's going to be more. Then I realize that there's not going to be any of that, because Cody and I are going to take care of it.

Over the complete chaos, I spot Rocky and consider going to her, but then I remember that she's probably the betrayer, and I'm the betrayee.

So I stand absolutely still without moving.

I also realize that since Cody and I are going to be going to the Government Building, I don't have to do the Poverty round in the Trial. It doesn't even matter anymore since the Elector's going to drug us all with sleeping serum.

Then I think to myself, *How did all that information even get into my dream/nightmare, anyway?*

But that's a question even Cody might not be able to answer.

Cody might be the city's--or even *world's* most notorious Criminal, but he's pretty smart. He even figured out the deal with the triangle tattoos, that it might be the symbol of the Disparate.

I want to scream--Everything is so confusing, and I'm having trouble processing this. All of my classmates, friends, are going to have to fight against each other now, kill each other. If I were to be in the round, which I'm not, even Rocky would have no choice but to put me to my death.

I don't wait for anything else to happen. I just run straight to my room, slam the door behind me, rip off my bag, stuff my face with a pillow, and scream. I scream so badly that after I remove the pillow from my face, my throat feels sore. The screaming doesn't seem to help. Mascao once told me that it was okay to let your feelings out, as long as you're alone, or you're with someone you love and trust.

The thought of Mascao makes me want to cry now. Everything's going to change now. Mascao and I won't be having the pleasant memories I had when I was seven years old. We are going to move on in life, away, away from the past, and more into the future.

PART 2
BREAK-IN

CHAPTER 28

N ow all we have to do is come up with the right time and place
to meet up for the attack.

Since I don't have anything else to do, I decide to take a walk.
Maybe some other idea will come to me while I walk around the
neighborhood of Versa Sector.

As I step outside of the school, I overhear some commotion and
realize that one of the mentors is talking. I quickly step back inside
and shuffle past the secretary and into the Lounge. Trying to keep
hidden, I listen to the mentor continue.

"We're going to be starting the next round of the Trial," he says.
"A lot of you guys might not be happy. I've spoken with the Senate to
set this up for you guys. So, here it is…" Silence. "You're going to be
sent to Poverty."

And that's when I leave. I don't want to hear anything else they're
planning to put April in danger.

Even though April's going to escape the Trial anyway, it worries
me how many people are dying because of the Elector.

I curse the Elector under my breath as I speed walk outside
into the morning sun. It seems pretty quiet in the Versa Sector this
morning, because there are no aircars speeding by with rushed
workers driving to work. Suspicion crawls through me and I raise
an eyebrow, shoving my hands into my pockets and start to casually
stroll along the sidewalk.

In all the houses I pass by it seems that they're all empty. A JumboTron is flashing some news in front of me: PAIRING CEREMONY TODAY. ALL STUDENTS 15 YEARS MUST REPORT TO THE PAIRING CENTER FOR THEIR PAIRING.

This message confuses me for a little bit. Then I realize that the fifteen-year-olds aren't going to be there because they're at their Trials. Now everyone else is going to be held captive in the Versa Hall and while they wonder where the "Pairing Ceremony" is, the soldiers are going to lock the people in the building so they couldn't get out, thus taking control over everything because there are no adults helping attack the Elector, just the fifteen-year-olds.

Rage makes me want to break something, so I go to the nearest (empty) store and smash open the window, hopping inside the large gaping hole. It turns out to be a computer store, so I grab all the the computers on display and smash them against the tables. I don't stop until I'm surrounded by bits of computer pieces and every single electronic thing is destroyed in the small store. Satisfied, I continue to stroll casually along the sidewalk with my hands in my pockets.

I'm on my way back to Jeff.

CHAPTER 29

I stay in my room for the rest of the day, occasionally sneaking downstairs to the Food Bar to grab a snack. I don't move at all from my bed, and I read a little from my book, and experiment new hairstyles. It's a girl thing. You boys wouldn't understand.

I also brainstorm. When we should attack the Government Building, how we should get Mascao out, and, most important of all, how we get to the Elector President.

Maybe we could scale the Building. But then I realize that no, it would take us too much time and energy, because we need the energy to fight when we need to.

Then I consider talking to Rocky about this. I think of how our conversation will/would be:

Me: "Rocky, I'm escaping the Trial."

Rocky: "WHAT?! ARE YOU CRAZY! You could get caught! Or worse! You could be Executed!"

Me: (smirks)

Rocky: "You're gonna do something crazy. I know it. I love crazy. WHAT IS YOUR PLAN MASTER?"

And then Rocky and I join Cody with breaking Mascao out of Execution and then we slay the Elector and then we live happily ever after, The End.

Sometimes I can't stand my ridiculous fantasies. The first line that Rocky says will be true of course, but I don't know if the second line will be true.

Then I think about how in all books the characters just stumble into crime or something terrible or whatever. Cody and I have everything very carefully planned. At The Beginning, I stumbled into Cody, Cody stumbled into Execution three years before, and that's how this all started. The Elector stumbled unto this land, and he stumbled into the idea of drugging the entire world so he can take over. How *quaint*.

I munch on an apple (I know I'm not allowed because of braces, but whatever) and untangle a failed attempt at making a bun from my hair. I run my fingers in through the thick brown hair to settle down the wild and frizzy parts that somehow formed while experimenting on the hairstyles.

After putting all my things away into the bag and finish off the apple, tossing it into a nearby trashcan while heading into the bathroom to take a shower. As the warm water runs over me, I think about how I missed today's first classes, and how I don't really care. I'm going to ditch the Trial anyway. But I'm also going to have to be careful while I go downstairs to the Food Bar to get food. Then I decide that after I finish taking a shower, I'll go to the Bar while everyone's sleeping and take all the food I need. I'll pack them in my bag, and sneak out of the school.

I step out of the shower, dry up and get dressed. I grab the bag that is sitting on my bed and search for what I need: a wrench.

Facing towards the mirror in the bathroom, I ready the wrench at my mouth and open wide to reveal my braces completely. I squish my eyes shut; I know this is going to hurt.

CHAPTER 30

We don't have that much time until the Elector takes over the world. It sounds terrible when you think about it, but it actually sounds impossible the more you consider it.

I just have to go get April.

Maybe I should wait until nighttime when everyone's sleeping. I'm sure April will know that the sooner, the better, and she'll somehow break out at night. After that we'll go get Mascao at the Execution Center. It might actually be easier at night since a lot of people end their shifts at that time.

This plan might just work.

I barely realize where I'm walking until I end up at the foot of the Government Building. Guards surround the entrance, but I'm far enough from them so they won't get suspicious. The tower looms way above the clouds, and I'm kind of scared to find out what's up there.

When I was twelve and still in school, my teacher Mrs. White would always correct us students whenever we said something like, "like" or "kind of". She would ask us a question, "What is a bough?" And one of us would answer, "It's kind of like a–" Then she would interrupt us and say, "Not 'kind of like'. It's…?" And the student would answer, "It *is* a branch on an evergreen tree." while smiling.

Now this reminds me to correct myself. I'm not *kind of scared* to go to the Government Building. I *am* scared to go to the Government Building. I hate to admit it, but it's true.

Today is cold, even though it's summer. I shove my hands into my pockets and breath out a long breath that I've probably held for a long time.

The Elector President wanted "his" people to experience nature itself in the boundaries of the city, but one day her found out how hot it really is here in the summer. People died of thirst, plants dried up, and almost everyone in the Senate was going on strike until the Elector did something about this. So then he installed an "air conditioner" to the Wall so it can cool the entire city. Sometimes it breaks down in the summer and it either gets freezing like now, or it becomes scorching hot.

I let out another breath and turn my back on the Building before gaping at the part where it disappears into the clouds.

CHAPTER 31

Night can't come any faster. I already packed my bag with everything I could. Before I slip out the door, I click off all of the lights and gently close the door behind me without making a sound.

I start down the hallway on tiptoes, but moving fast. At the stairs there's a glint of light still shining, so the fire must still be alive.

Just as I'm about the make my way down the stairs, someone grabs my shoulder and I start to scream but a hand goes over my mouth, muffling my scream.

"What are you doing?!" a voice hisses into my ear. I squirm out of their grasp and turn to face towards the direction where the voice came from. I gasp.

It's Rocky.

"The same question goes back to you!" I whisper-shout back to her.

"April, you're crazy! What you're trying to do is ridiculous! You're going to get yourself killed!"

I jerk myself away from Rocky and scowl at her.

"If you would listen to me, you would understand!" I sigh and pull on the collar of my shirt, revealing the triangle tattoo. Rocky gasps and covers her nose and mouth with her hands.

"What is this?" she asks. I sigh again and let go of the collar, hiding the tattoo again.

"This is the symbol of the Disparate," I explain to her. Rocky gasps again.

This time it's me who grabs Rocky by the shoulders. "Girl, get a hold of yourself!" I shake her around a couple of times until she has to stop me.

"Okay, okay," she says, "but explain more to me."

So I do. I tell her about the dream I had where the soldier told me everything, I told her about the Generator, and I told her how the Elector is bad, not good.

At the end Rocky has this look on her that tells me that she either is satisfied, or she really has to go.

"Are you satisfied?" I ask her.

Rocky nods. "Yeah, but I also *really* have to go."

I chuckle at her a little as she skitters down the hallway into her room.

"Oh, and by the way, I got my braces off," I half whisper as we tiptoe downstairs into the Lounge. Rocky peeks at me for evidence and I grin as big as I can. My teeth are good enough anyway. I don't need them,

"What?! Who?! Where?! When?! Why?! How?!" Rocky shouts.

"Shhh!" I shush Rocky. "I got my braces off. It's me. In my bathroom upstairs. Just before I left. Because I'm sick of them. And with a wrench." We sit down on the easy chairs. Rocky nods and goes on as if ripping your braces out is something you do every day.

"So, to shut down the entire city, we have to destroy the Generator?" Rocky questions me.

"Yeah, but we're going to have to find it," I reply. "Word says that it's so cleverly hidden that sometimes even the Elector President himself forgets where it is from time to time."

Rocky breathes a *whoa* and slumps back into her couch, munching on a cookie she got from the Food Bar.

There's silence for a little while except for the dying fire sizzling in the fireplace. Then suddenly Rocky sits abruptly sits up in her seat and tells me, "We have to get out of here before it's morning or someone else finds you, because you weren't in our first classes." I nod at her and get up, glancing at the un-eaten cookie that is still in Rocky's hand. Maybe I should eat, but I have absolutely no appetite ever since I stepped out of my room. I nod again.

"Okay, let's go." I take a deep breath. We're going to have to be careful, I assume. There's probably an alarm that's gonna go off the second we step out of this room."

Rocky strokes her chin in thought while shoving the rest of the cookie into her mouth. "We can break out of the door, run out of this place, and jump into the nearest dumpster."

"That's a good idea," I say, "Except for the dumpster part. Let's do it."

I start towards the door and am about to open it when Rocky calls out, "Cookie?"

"Nah," I answer. "No appetite."

"Well, I'm taking all." Rocky takes all of the cookies and drops them each into her shirt, using the bottom as a pocket.

"Aw, this is why I love you." I run over to Rocky and squeeze her into a hug.

"I would hug you back, but cookies are better," Rocky teases. "Better keep them all."

I grin. "Let's just get this over with."

Rocky cups the cookies safely in her shirt and we charge out of the Lounge with the alarm sounding almost immediately. We sprint past the secretary desk, out the front doors, down the stairs, and off into the night.

CHAPTER 32

A larms sound in the distance, towards the direction of the Versa Sector School. April must have broken out.

I start running at top speed towards the ear-piercing noise. It's getting darker by the second. I better hurry until it gets pitch-black.

The alarm is getting louder and louder, and I also hear some chattering and outbursts. I slow down as I reach the entrance. There's a crowd of people standing at the foot of the school. A woman approaches me.

"Excuse me," she says, "have you seen two girls? They're named April Ingalls and Rochelle Dale." I freeze. Has Rocky decided to come along with April?

I hesitate. "No…" The woman gives me a suspicious look.

"You hesitated. No one's allowed to hesitate here. You look a little familiar." The woman examines me closer as I hold my breath. "You're…" And then she yells at the top of her lungs, "IT'S CODY VARES!"

My heart starts to pound faster as everyone in the crowd turns their attention to me.

I back up a little.

Then I start to run.

This is kind of like deja vu. I was chased multiple times in the past three years. Today reminds me of that day I was captured by those silver-suit dudes. Someone recognizes me, they're going to catch me and throw me into Execution. But this is not one of those moments where there's just one person who recognizes me and chases after me until they tire out. This is an entire mob chasing after me. These people really hate me. But I'm used to hatred. I remember in school I was always teased for the irregular color of my eyes. Some kids would say, "Everyone back off! The kid with the endless pit in his eyes is coming! Don't look or you'll be sucked in!" And everyone will look into my eyes and pretend to be drawn towards me while howling with laughter.

I've never run this fast in my entire life. Some people might say that I'm running for my life. Technically, I'm not really running for my life. You could say that I'm running for the Elector, for April, for Mom and Dad.

I'm running so fast, the only thing that I'm concentrating on is to not trip. I don't notice an arm popping out in front of me behind a building. The arm grabs me and pulls me towards the back of the building at such force and quickness that the angry mob doesn't even know that I've disappeared.

It takes me a moment to realize where I am when the voice of April hisses, "There you are!" I'm still kind of dazed from the impact, so I sit down, my back against the brick wall of the building.

"Honestly, I can't believe how much those people can't stand you," says another voice. "It's like, 'Hi, I'm a notorious so-called Criminal for doing absolutely nothing!' And then, 'Oh my gosh, you're a notorious so-called Criminal for doing absolutely nothing? We better get you and kill you!'"

"I think you dislocated my shoulder," I pipe up randomly. Just as I say it, a jolt of pain travels up my arm.

April scoffs. "How?"

"Um, inertia," I reply. "Aren't you going to help me?"

"Oh, right. I think I have a first aid kit in here…" April opens up her bag and scours through it a little bit before presenting a first aid kit that looks like it's barely been touched. She opens it up and I look up to find where the other voice is coming from. It takes me a moment to recognize the person as she sits down, her legs stretched out and her back against the wall, munching on a chocolate chip cookie. It's Rocky with her brown and blue curly hair bounces as she nods to the beat of a song she's listening to on her mini TouchPad.

I stare at her as April takes my arm, cradling it gently in her hand before straightening it out and jerking it up. I feel the bones of my shoulder grinding against each other as they shift back into place and I scream from the pain before April clamps her hand over my mouth.

"Stop trying to draw attention!" she spits at me. I roll my eyes at her, struggling with the urge to not cry. But I don't want to cry in front of two girls. It'll make me look like a baby.

April takes some cream from the first aid kit and squirts some on her hand, slips off my jacket, pulls up the sleeve of my t-shirt, and spreads the cream on my shoulder where it was dislocated. After a few seconds my shoulder gets warm and the pain eases a little bit. I smile gratefully at April and cover myself with the jacket again.

I glance at Rocky as she keeps bobbing her head to the music. I decide to reach over and ask her, "Can I have a cookie?" Rocky rips off the ear buds and shoves the mini TouchPad in her pocket. She takes one cookie that was settled in her shirt and hands it to me. I hastily gobble down the cookie and stand up.

"Okay." I take a deep breath. "Let's go to the Execution Center. Most people probably already ended their shifts, so it's going to be easier to break Mascao out."

Rocky nods. "Yeah, but first, I want to do something to show that I'm rebelling against the Government." She grabs the hair elastic at the bottom of her ponytail and pulls on it to let her hair out. Rocky flips it over and back a couple of times and grins at me and April. Soon, April does the same to her bun, carefully taking out the bobby pins and throwing them to the ground along with the hair elastic.

I watch the two of them giggling to each other and watching me. Maybe they're expecting me to do something that will show that I'm rebelling against the Elector President, the Government, the Senate. So I decide to satisfy them and take off my jacket again, dropping it into my bag, ripping off a piece of the collar of my t-shirt to completely show the tattoo of the Disparate.

CHAPTER 33

The three of us run nonstop towards the direction of the Government Building with the broken AC System making the night air chilly.

I don't know why Cody has thought of the idea to ditch his jacket and show off his tattoo. It's kind of stupid to run around without a jacket, especially at night. So I guess Cody really likes getting the flu or a cold.

From time to time Cody has to look around the corner of a block to check if the angry mob is there. This annoys me so much that it makes me want to grab him and yell at him, "You don't have to be a hero now, Cody Dalton Vares! We can take care of ourselves!" But willpower prevents me from doing that.

The city is actually not that big when you think about it. I guess it's just because I've lived here my entire life.

I've never really craved the idea of escaping the city. It hasn't really come into my mind actually. I've never thought of breaking through the wall just like how I somehow broke it in the dream. But now when I think about it, it suddenly makes me want to get out of here so badly that I'm shaking with anticipation every time we pause so Cody can do the mob-check thing.

It's kind of weird to daydream while you're running, because it's like you're asleep, but your body is moving. It's also hard to concentrate on the running, and it's a good thing Rocky noticed, because whenever we have to make a turn, Rocky takes hold of me and swerves me towards the direction we have to go to.

I have never noticed that we've entered the Poor Sector, but you can obviously realize that it's completely different from the other sectors, because there are wrappers and all that stuff all over the ground. It also seems like it's become darker. There are people in ragged clothing walking around and eyeballing us. We slow down to fast walking as Cody maneuvers us to random directions. I feel really uncomfortable, so I grab Rocky's arm and squeeze super hard. She yelps a little, but awkwardly pats me on my shoulder back to return the gesture.

Now that we're in the Poor Sector, it's weird to know that such an "important" building is in such an "unimportant" area.

I *really* don't want to say that I'm scared, because all these people have lived here their entire lives, and they're used to it, but I've lived in the Versa Sector my entire life also, so I kind of feel like a spoiled brat. These people probably could kill to live in the class that I'm currently in.

"Cody," Rocky says, breaking our silence, "this place is creepy. *Get us out!*"

Cody nods absently, turning us towards a small white building with glass windows surrounding it and a small sign that marks *Execution Center*. He opens the door for us and Rocky pulls me inside without saying thank you.

The Execution Center is way more better-looking on the inside, and all the dark thoughts that swirled through my head involving one of those creepy homeless people out there stabbing me disappeared.

There's no one behind the reception desk except for some military guy. I'm actually really scared right now, because it seems like everyone is acting like zombies.

Then this terrifying thought strikes me.

"I think we're too late," I whisper.

Maybe this isn't a sleeping serum that the Elector is drugging the people with. It could be a mind washing serum.

The soldier just sits there without blinking as the three of us freeze in place, trying not to breath.

To make matters worse, one of the lights are broken, and it blinks and buzzes to freak me out even more.

Cody tries to ignore the military guy and pulls us through a door that was behind the soldier. He doesn't move.

Just before disappear through the door and it shuts behind us, I realize that the soldier is Mascao.

CHAPTER 34

I hear a click just as the door shuts that makes me jump a little. I turn back to twist the doorknob a couple of times but it won't budge.

We're locked in.

Rocky screams with fright and I will myself not to roll my eyes at her. If I were a girl I would probably scream too. April stays silent, being the different girl she is, and looks up at me.

"That was Mascao," she tells me.

"I know," I reply, even though I don't. I grab her arm. "*Run!*"

All three of us bolt towards the other direction and I grab the doorknob of a random door and push Rocky and April inside. It turns out that it's one of those offices where the Executioners discuss whether they should Execute the person or not. I slam the door behind me and Rocky starts screaming again.

"*Shh!*" April and I hiss at her. She cuts off almost immediately and April says, "But what about Mascao?"

"We can't go get him. He's under some drug," I explain to her.

"No. We can't go without Mascao! We came here to get him!"

"It's too dangerous! We don't know what's out there!"

"But he's the only family I have left!" April glares at me and I fall silent.

During the silence, I hear footsteps coming this way. And they're coming fast.

"Hide!" I whisper-shout at the girls and duck underneath the desk. They do the same and each of us hold our breath until the footsteps fade.

"Now what?" April mouths at me. I ponder for an idea.

"Maybe I should start acting like you, and we let ourselves be found," I whisper back. "We want to get into the Building, remember? They might as well take us there into prison, because the Execution Center is no use any more."

April nods approvingly. "Yeah, that would be very me-like. But I'd rather we get out of here and go straight towards the Government Building. Like ninjas."

"But--" I start to say, but April interrupts me by giving me a nasty look, telling me to shut up until it's all over.

Rocky starts to shake and April scooches over to her to hug Rocky. I stay where I am to ponder about what we should do. Doing April's plan would take a very long time. It's one hundred stories. *One hundred stories.* Even I couldn't scale that, after some time of climbing during those three years, not to brag.

But April's plan could also be the safest plan. If soldiers or agents capture us, they could do a little damage to us, like redislocate my shoulder or give us concussions.

But if they capture us, we would probably go unconscious and it would take very little time for us to get to the top.

But they probably wouldn't bring us immediately to the top. They could even bring us to a prison at the first floor. It would take us forever to get to the top.

I shake my head with disappointment, and get up, grab the nearest heavy object, (a stapler) and throw it towards the office window.

April and Rocky duck lower underneath the desk as glass shoots everywhere.

I don't really care as the little glass bits cut into my skin as alarms blare throughout the Execution Center.

Rocky's lips start to quiver and April shoots a nasty look at me. I shrug.

"Let's get out of here!" Rocky screeches. The girls start to get up and run towards the broken window, but I stop them by blocking the gaping hole in the window.

"Let. Us. Out." April grits her teeth and gives me an even nastier look.

"No." I cringe a little because I know that April wouldn't be afraid to beat me until I beg for mercy.

"*Pour l'amour du ciel! Laissez-nous sortir de la salle! Je ne veux pas rester ici plus! Dieu, Dieu, Dieu, pourquoi ai-je accepte de le faire? Avec vous, surtout! Je vous deteste!* Ugh!" Rocky's eyes go wide with fright and stares at me worriedly.

"She yells French when she's mad," Rocky explains.

"What did she say?"

"Something about hating you, about letting us out, about not wanting to sit here anymore, blah, blah, blah. She could yell at you in more languages."

"*Co to ma znaczyc? Dlaczego, dlaczego! Ja bym chciala isc do domu i zachowywac sie jakby nic sie nie stalo! Oh ja Boga! Dlaczego?*"

"Now what was that?"

"Polish. Pretend like nothing's happening."

But things are happening.

The last things I see are soldiers bursting into the room and the girls screaming.

CHAPTER 35

I open my eyes. I'm lying in the middle of the street, but no aircars are floating over me.

I wipe my face with the sleeves of my jacket and stand up. There's a mob of people standing around me, forming a large circle where I am standing in the middle. Silver cars block out the mob from coming into the circle, and men in silver suits stand around talking amongst themselves and into walkie talkies. The people in the mob are whispering frantically. I look around me to find that I am completely surrounded. I can't get out.

Above all the chattering I hear the whirring of a helicopter all of a sudden. I glance up to the sky and a ladder drops down onto me. The helicopter hovers for above me, and people are shouting with anger.

For a second I'm confused, and then I realize that the helicopter is my chance to escape.

I step onto the last bar of the ladder and grip the bar above me for dear life as the helicopter slowly lifts me from the ground.

As I look down to the empty circle, I notice that nobody's doing anything about my escape. They just start to panic, and chaos happens.

People run towards all directions, they're shielding their heads, they're rushing to the men in silver suits and begging them to do something about my escape.

Some people are running to random buildings and slamming the doors behind them.

They're really scared of me, *I think to myself.*

The helicopter rises higher and higher, but I'm not scared at all, hence my fear of heights.

I smile to myself, even though I know I'm not supposed to. These people are completely out of order. They have no idea what to do when something bad happens. Like they should go into lockdown if the city's most notorious Criminal is attacking the Diamond Sector or something.

Then I gasp.

I'm *the city's most notorious Criminal now.*

I'm Cody.

I hear shouting above me and look up to see a young man with long black hair tied up in a ponytail with gray baggy pants and a black sweatshirt waving me over.

"Get over here!" he yells at me. "We have plenty of time to finally get to the top of the Government Building. Those people don't know how to control things properly. By the time they'll start to try to attack us, we'll be long gone in Nalaska City."

I nod and scramble up the ladder, climbing into the helicopter with the help of the man's hand pulling me up.

"All right, Cody. Grab a gun or whatever, and we're off."

"We?" I sit against the wall of the helicopter and look to see a guy with huge glasses and the same outfit as the dude who helped me up inside steering the helicopter.

"Yeah. There's brainy Brian over there, and then there's me." The guy in the glasses turns to us for half a second to see if I'm here and turns back to steering.

"Shut up, Cole. I'm not a nerd," Brian pipes up.

"You might as well be one." Cole strolls over to Brian and slaps him on the shoulder.

Brian might look embarrassed, but underneath all that embarrassment I saw a smile creep up on his lips.

"Okay. Cody, you better get a good weapon if you want to kill the Elector. Like, right away." Cole opens up a trunk in the back of the helicopter and pulls out a huge gun that I can't identify, but Cody probably can, because Cole's got this huge stupid grin on his face. He hands it over to me.

"You're welcome," he scoffs proudly.

"Wait," I start, *"I'm supposed to kill the Elector? How am I supposed to use this thing? It's bigger than my upper body. Where is the Elector? What's going on?"*

"Boy, you really are clueless today," Cole sighs and takes the gun from me.

"Shut up, Cole," Brian repeats. *"He probably has some temporary amnesia from when that agent conked him in the head."*

"'Temporary amnesia'? And you, my man, are a nerd."

"Shut up."

"Okay!" Cole cuts the conversation. *"I'll show you how to use this baby, if you really do have temporary amnesia."*

I nod.

"Yes, as in you do have temporary amnesia? Or yes, you want me to show you how to use this?"

"Yes, I want you to show me how to use that." I roll my eyes. Cole is really annoying me.

"Don't roll your eyes at me."

"I didn't say I did."

"Of course you don't say it! You see it."

"I didn't roll my eyes."

"YES YOU DID! I saw you roll those bleeping *eyes!"(I'm censoring the swears. Sorry)*

"SHUT UP!" Brian shouts, and Cole and I shut up. *"Just show him how to use the stupid gun!"*

"You know what? I can handle this thing myself." I rip the heavy gun out of Cole's hands. If I were me, I wouldn't be able to even rip the

thing out of his hands. It's so heavy. But in Cody's body, he has these huge biceps, so handling the gun is no big deal.

"Show us, then. When we get to the Government Building, you show us shooting the Elector President right in the bleeping *head. You dig?" Cole crosses his arms.*

"Fine!"

We all fall silent, with Brian still steering the helicopter and Cole standing next to him with a hand on his shoulder, as if Brian was his son, and he was the proud dad. I smile a little bit, knowing that it will look like Cody's smirk that he has on almost all the time.

Brian finally steers the helicopter towards the top of the Government Building.

It isn't what I imagined it would be.

It looks like paradise--the Elector is sprawled out on a lounging chair dressed in khakis and a button-up shirt with sunglasses and a fancy drink in his hand and butlers standing next to him in case he ordered something to them.

I gasp a little.

"What are you, a girl? Shoot the bleeping bleep!*" Cole screamed at me. "Show us what you got! Don't you let us down, Cody Dalton Vares!"*

At first I'm surprised at Cole for yelling Cody's full name at me with such passion.

I nervously aim at the Elector with the huge gun, squishing one eye shut and resting my finger on the trigger.

And I shoot.

CHAPTER 36

I open my eyes. I'm lying in the middle of the street, but no aircars are floating over me.

Wiping the sleep from my eyes, I stand up and scan my background.

It's a neighborhood. A huge white mansion stands in front of me. Or rather, it doesn't stand. It floats. A long gleaming white staircase is stretched out in front of me, leading to the house.

It doesn't have any beams to lean on. I guess it's floating, too.

I look around me, and realize that there aren't any more houses, or mansions. It's kind of foggy, and it's very quiet. The only area that is clear is the white mansion.

The mansion reminds me of an ancient mansion that is now a museum. It's called the White House. It was burned down in the World War IV when Australia invaded the United States. It was a home to all the leaders of the United States. They were called presidents. Since it was burned down, builders tried to rebuild the White House completely.

I have never visited the White House because it's too far away from where I live and my family and I never were able to afford transportation.

It takes me a moment to figure out that I'm supposed to go inside the mansion.

As I step onto the first stair and make my way upstairs, I take note of the large hedges covering the backyard. They're perfectly trimmed, so this place must be carefully taken care of.

The sound of rushing water comes from a fountain of an angel standing on a pedestal with water spraying out in all directions.

I finally get to the last stair, and I cautiously open the door.

The first thing I hear is chattering. Then the sound of a classical piano playing a tune. I can't recognize it, but I think it's really old.

I open the door wider and spot a man dressed in a really fancy suit sitting formally before a large black piano and pressing the keys lightly.

There's a chandelier hanging from the ceiling, glittering marvelously in the light and a crisp clean marble floor showing my reflection. I step inside, gently shutting the door behind me.

"Good evening, Madame," a voice says to me. I look up to see a butcher standing there in front of me with a hand behind his back as he bows deeply to me.

I jump a little, startled, before I blush profusely. "I'm not a girl."

The butcher suddenly looks surprised. "Of course you are, Madame Ingalls. Are you feeling alright? I must fetch you a drink of water. You look sickly."

My eyes go wide. I'm April? A girl? I furrow my eyebrows at him.

"As a matter of fact, I do feel a cold coming. I must rest in my beloved room where I shall shut my eyes in sleep."

I almost burst out laughing like a hyena. I've never spoken that way before. I sounded like a princess.

Before I leave to go to my "bedroom"/explore a little bit more, I do a deep curtsy at the butcher and smirk at myself as I stare at my knees. My girly knees. When I stand again, the butcher looks surprised. Or, should I say, flabbergasted. Like a pretty little princess.

He clears his throat. "Well, then, I have a thought that I must take care of Lily at the moment. She is quite fretful." Lily. Whoever that is.

I start to snicker, but I cover it up with a fake cough. "I must be going." I start towards the huge marble staircase that stands next to the piano, and watch out of the corner of my eyes as the butcher returns to playing the piano. Just as he starts to play a tune, I swish my head towards him and narrow my eyes. The butcher goes wide-eyed and frantically starts playing a song that apparently I like. I'm just screwing with him. I kind of feel special now. I grin as I carefully step up the stairs, just like a princess.

This actually feels awkward, because, well, I'm a girl. *I don't even know what I'm supposed to do. Am I supposed to go over to a slumber party with friends and giggle about boys all night? I literally have no experience with this kind of stuff. Sure, I have two little sisters, but my family's poor, so basically we're more concentrated on staying inside and not do anything stupid that could get us Executed than going over to friends' houses and playing tag or watching a movie or whatever.*

As I finally step up to the top (the stairs are sooo long like OMG. That's what girls say, right?), a hand grabs onto my shoulder and shoves me into a room with such force I bet it could dislocate my shoulder. Again.

The door to the room is slammed behind me and I quickly spot a large queen-sized bed covered in a canopy, and flop down onto it.

I hear someone squeal behind me.

"OMG! OMG. I saw what you did Appy! That was so suave! OMG! I wish I could do that! OMG! OMG! His eyeballs almost popped out of his tiny head! And I was like: OMG! OMG! OMG! I watched everything from the balcony! I mean, it's like: TTYL! LOL! OMG!" Arms squeeze me into a tight hug and I almost gag. I'm not used to emotion and love, even though I have a family.

Okay, let me just say, I have never heard anyone say OMG that much in one statement. I guess girls have the power to make that happen.

"Calm down," I choke out. I swear to God, this girl is trying to strangle me.

"Oh, am I hurting you? I'm sorry, Appy. Now let's get ready for the part-ay."

I turn to face the girl who almost killed me via hugging. Now my *eyes almost pop out of my head.*

It's Rocky.

"Which dress do you want?" Rocky turns to me with the most disgusting pink girly dress I have ever seen in my life. Then I smirk. I'm not a boy now. I'm a girl, and no one would tell that a boy is actually wearing a pink floral dress up to the knees with no straps that would probably make me look half naked.

"IDK," I decide to try out. It feels weird, saying abbreviations for sentences you can easily say. "You choose. I don't care tonight. Just not pink."

"Yeah, you're right." Rocky turns back to the closet she was digging through. "Pink is so retarted."

I almost sigh with relief. I hate pink. I hate hate hate pink. Who came up with the color, I don't know. And yes, I should care, because if I get my hands on one of those time machines the Elector keeps in the Government Building, I'll go back in time and kill the guy. Or girl.

Speaking of the Government Building...

"Rocky," I say, "Where's Cody? We should probably get on with our mission. You know? Government Building, Elector President is evil..." I let myself trail off and stare up at Rocky, trying to make innocent-looking eyes.

"What are you talking about?" Rocky finally answers. "Cody is coming to the part-ay, though. And you know you've have a crush on him since, like, forever. This is your big chance, Appy!"

I have to paste this big, stupid smile on my face to keep myself from throwing up all over the floor.

Later at the party, I'm dressed in a pale blue dress that is, yes, up to my knees, and also, with no straps.

Great.

I'm also covered in the most makeup I've ever had on in my entire life, not like I've had any on before. When Rocky begged me for her to do my makeup, I said yes, but to go easy on the blush and eyeshadow to make it look "natural".

In the mansion, there's this special room called the "ballroom". When I got there, I thought that I would see everyone playing with a ball. I know, laugh at me. It's actually a dance room. Where you dance. *Dancing the funniest thing, right? People flail their arms, kick their legs, and worst of all, there's slow dancing. Rocky tells me the more proper name is the "waltz". I think it's just darn right stupid. And seeing me in a tuxedo putting my hands on another chick's waist, like right near her butt, makes me want to go up there to myself and punch me.*

"Impossible," I mutter under my breath just as Rocky walks up to me.

"Nothing's impossible, Appy!" she says to me cheerfully. "After all, we're in a floating mansion!"

True, true, I think and go up to the refreshments bar to grab a drink.

As I sip on the blood-red punch, I scan my surroundings to see who's dancing with whom.

The slow song ends, an the DJ puts on an upbeat song that gets everybody dancing excitedly and the girls returning to their groups. Technically, the way I'm seeing it right now, the dancefloor is divided into two groups: the girls on one half, giggling about who she danced with, and the boys on the other half, clapping each other's backs, showing pride to the guy who supposedly danced with some hot girl. And I just realize that only when a slow song comes on is when the boys and girls mingle.

Since I have like no friends, I stay at the refreshments bar, eating all the snacks, but mostly drinking the punch, and then having to go to the bathroom (let me just say, the first time I went to the bathroom I accidentally went into the mens' room, out of habit, and the guy in there was probably some guy from school who was madly in love with me, and he didn't even mind me being in there, he acted as if it was the most normal thing ever before he pushed me against the wall, locked the door, and leaned in to kiss me. I slapped him, of course, and got out of there as soon as possible, to escape into the womens' room, and lock the door).

By the time I got back from the fifth trip to the bathroom to the ballroom and the refreshments table, another slow song was on, and lots of people were already paired up.

I grab another cup of punch and start to gulp it down again when me, yes, me, came over to the refreshments table right next to me, and grabbed one of those finger sandwich thingies.

"Hi," not-Cody says out of the blue, which makes me jump, startled. And I thought he didn't see me!

"'Sup," I try to reply as casually as possible. I stare at the bottom of my cup of punch and look up to see Rocky popping up from the crowd of dancing people, giving me the thumbs-up. I feel myself redden and look down, remembering that the room is dark, and that not-Cody probably can't see me, so I look back up to face him. He's grinning stupidly.

No, I think worriedly as not-Cody flips his hair back attractively. *But I smile a little, not at him, but at myself, realizing how utterly adorable and handsome I am, and wondering why I still don't have a girlfriend.* Oh yeah, *I think again,* I'm a notorious Criminal, and everybody hates my guts.

Then not-Cody interrupts my thoughts by saying, "So, um, you want to dance?" and I almost spit out the huge gulp of punch I just filled up in my mouth.

"Me?" I manage to squeak out, still choking on the punch.

"You okay?" not-Cody asks me worriedly, changing the subject abruptly.

"Yeah, sure."

"Anywaaaaaaaaay." Not-Cody goes on firmly. "Dance. You. Me. Now. Okay?"

I grin from ear to ear. Classical Cody-picking-up-girls-method– Say each word as a sentence. Works every time.

"Sure," I reply, still grinning.

Not-Cody grins back and takes my hand, leading me towards the dancefloor, away from the refreshments table. We stand somewhere in the middle of the dancefloor, and not-Cody puts his hands on my waist, and from watching all those people slow-dancing with each other, I now know that I'm supposed to put my hands at his shoulders, so I do.

"I don't know how to dance, though," I whisper to not-Cody.

"You just kinda, shuffle your feet from side to side," not-Cody whispers back.

And so we dance.

It super awkward, so the whole time I sort of just stare out into the open, not sure where else to look.

I can hear other girls giggling and talking with their dance partner, so I start to giggle stupidly and nervously too. It's actually not that hard to giggle, it just comes naturally. I always thought that giggling was the hardest thing ever to do.

Just as the song ends, and nobody's looking at us because they're too busy hugging their partners, I look up at not-Cody, thinking that's what I'm supposed to do, but instead, he leans in and presses his lips against mine.

CHAPTER 37

I wake, up screaming, shuddering violently as the last scene keeps coming and going through my mind.

Normally, the idea of me making out with myself would be beautiful, because I'm basically a guy with high self-esteem, but this is me making out with myself as a *girl*.

Trying to slow down my breathing, I scan my surroundings to see where I was sleeping. Was this all a dream?

Wait a minute.

White sterile walls.

Glaring white lights.

No windows.

I'm back in the Operation Room.

CHAPTER 38

ow did I ever get back in here? I want to sob. I want to scream. Punch something, kill someone, anything. This is a building where they bring so-called "Criminals" in to kill them because they've done one thing, *one thing* wrong.

I've also heard that sometimes they are spared.

But also tortured.

The Executioners experiment on the people they think are "interesting". They would stick in needles with God knows what inside them, operate surgeries on the "experiment's" brain to see if they can "improve" them.

I know that by now you must be thinking, "Cody, I can hear your sarcasm from miles away."

Well, not to brag, but I speak fluent Sarcasm.

I decide that instead of getting up and pacing around the room like last time, I would hide under the bed, or covers.

I lean over the bed and glance down under the bed, only to find that the bed is not a bed, but just a large mattress.

"Ugh," I mutter to myself, also with some other very bad words that I shall not describe to you. I sit back up and duck underneath the covers, grateful to be away from those *awful*, glaring white lights. I curl up into a ball underneath the blanket, and pray.

Now usually, I'm not a very religious person, but I do believe in God and the Will of Testament and stuff like that. I pray whenever I'm in a tough situation like this. I also pray before I go to bed, things like, *Please don't let someone kill me tonight. I'm innocent, I swear.*

This time I pray as if my life depends on it. Well, technically, it does, but this time it's for real. I do *not* want to be experimented on. I don't think anybody does.

I mumble underneath the covers in prayer as if I've gone crazy when I hear the kind-of-familiar whooshing sound of the door to the Operation room opening and closing. I bite my lip and squish my eyes shut as I listen cautiously to the tapping of the footsteps coming towards me.

"Congratulations," a woman's voice tells me. "You passed the first test."

Wait, whaaaaaaaaaaaaaat? I scream in my head. A test?! What test?!

"What?" I manage to squeak out, still underneath the covers.

"Come out of there, Vares," the woman says.

I throw the covers off of me and find myself staring at the woman who I saw last time, in the office.

"Hi Cody." The woman smiles. "I'm Dr. Juliette Harper Caprison. Just call me Julie. Do you remember me?"

Yes, I remember her. I remember her throwing a skit party to get me to think I've actually committed a Crime, but I didn't. I'm *innocent*!

"Cody, I'm sure you have plenty of questions," Julie continues. "And I'm going to answer your first question. The reason why your back in the Operation room is because you never left it. Everything you've just experienced the past two years was all a dream."

Silence with my mouth open in horror. I hesitate a little before replying, "Whoa, okay, you got me there."

"I'm not lying, Cody," Julie goes on sharply. "We've made a kind of serum to put you into a coma that we have programmed to be for two years. We wanted to study you more, for you are Disparate, yes?

Remember how Dr. Tyler Black inserted that needle into your arm before our encounter in the office?"

I don't want to answer, but I need answers to what just happened. I nod.

"That was the serum. Our encounter in the office was just a dream. We all programmed it into the serum. We designed that serum just for you."

I don't know if that was supposed to make me feel better. It's like, "Oh, don't be so sad, because the bright side to this is that we made this horrible drug just for you! We spent so much time on it, don't you just love it?"

"Wait, so April...?"

"Yes, Cody. April was just a dream. We created her to be in your dream so it would seem real. You didn't decide the 'mission' to eliminate the Elector, we did. Everything you have just experienced the past few years was fake."

CHAPTER 39

W hat kind of horrible information is she going to tell me now, that I'm growing horns? I'm expecting her to come back into the Operation room any second now and tell me, "Oh, and that reminds me, while you were in your coma, we put in moose DNA into your blood, so you're growing horns!"

Minutes pass, but for me it feels like days. Since there are no windows, or at least those metal bar things they have in jail, I can't get out.

So I pace around the room. I can't think of an escape plan, and I'm not tired, so what else do I do?

After what feels like hours, not minutes, I hear the whooshing of the door opening and closing, and two people step in.

The first person is, well, you guessed it, Dr. Juliette Harper Caprison.

The second person is what I know you would never guess.

It's April.

CHAPTER 40

I can't do anything else but glare at her as a chair slides out of the wall and she sits down, crossing her legs formally. She tips the side of her hat that she's wearing in greeting.

"Hello, Cody," she says in an annoying formal voice. "Do you remember me? I acted as the dimwitted high school girl whom you met with one night. My name is Dr. April Christina Ingalls."

"I know," I growl at her, clenching my hands into fists. "I thought you were fake. I'd love for you to be fake. right now. You traitor."

April stares at me with fake surprise. "Me? Traitor? Why, Cody, I was never a traitor. But, I was also never your friend. I have only starred as the young woman you would meet while you were committing serious Crimes. I've always worked here. I finished elementary school at the age of three, and I whizzed through high school at the age of 12. So now here I am." April smiles at me sweetly, which makes me want to strangle her more. She reaches over towards the wall on her left, and a large blue bowl slides out of the wall. April reaches into the bowl and pulls out a chocolate chip cookie, crunching on it thoughtfully.

"You should really have one of these cookies," she says to me, still smiling. "They're really good."

I swat away the cookie out of her hand as she hands it over to me. "Thanks, but no thanks."

April looks like she might cry for a second, but then she regains her composure. I'm afraid I might have to interrogate you, Cody. Please have a seat." April gestures towards the wall opposite her, and I realize that the bed is gone, and a flimsy silver chair with armrests is replaced.

"No thanks," I reply coldly, crossing my arms. "I'd rather stand."

"Have I not made myself clear?" April asks me, with a little bit of impatience in her voice. "Please have a seat."

"Can I sit on the ground?" I question April with an annoying high-pitched voice I use whenever I'm stalling for time.

"Are you sure about that, Cody? The chair is much comfier."

"Yeah, I'm pretty sure. Those armrests could have arm straps in them to keep me from 'escaping'."

"Fine then." April flicks her wrist at Julie. "Take away the chair. Maybe we'll find a fabulous chair almost as good as this one, only without armrests. Cody would definitely enjoy that one. Also, maybe Cody would also enjoy some food. Because obviously Cody does not have a sweet tooth."

Julie nods obediently and taps some things into the TouchPad she has in her hands. Almost immediately the chair disappears and is replaced with a normal flimsy chair without armrests. A plate of bread with butter and a little chicken leg sits next to the chair on the ground. This makes me feel much better.

I grab the plate (without any silverware, by the way) and comfortably sit down on the chair.

April smiles again at me digging into the food and glances over at Julie. "You can leave now."

"Ah, yes, contact me if you need anything." Julie nods again and turns around on her heel, leaving the room with the whooshing of the wall/door opening and closing.

Julie leaving like that makes me wonder how powerful April is that she can make people twice as old as her leave the room without arguing.

"Okay, Cody," April turns back to me with a smile on her face. "I want to make this 'interrogation' private, so I had my workers to disable the cameras in here."

This statement makes me gulp down my piece of bread painfully. "What?"

April stops smiling, which makes me nervous for a second. This is the first time I've seen April so serious.

"First things first. I'm going to break you out of here, Cody. We *will* get the Elector President. We *must* save the city. Maybe even the world.

The truth is, everything that you just experienced in the coma was, sort of, real. There *is* the Generator, Cody. And we must destroy it. For two years, I've been watching you in your coma, and I realized, that the world *is* in danger."

CHAPTER 41

M y last statement kind of leaves Cody hanging there with his mouth open, so I decide to keep talking.

"I'll answer some of your questions, but here's the answer to the first: the person who captured you and brought you to the Execution Center was Mascao, my brother." I look down sadly for a moment, knowing how Mascao is still one of Them. The Senate.

Cody still looks shocked, so I'll just keep going.

"They wanted to see how you'd react when you'll hear what the Elector President really is doing. They thought that since you already knew the Elector was bad, it wouldn't matter if they revealed you the secret. Because...They were going to kill you anyway." I see Cody shudder violently, but I pretend I didn't notice.

"There *is* a Generator. The Elector President *is* planning to take over the world. That's why we need to stop him.

"Now to surprise you a little bit. They wanted to kill you *unless* their experiment worked on you. But if the experiment worked, they would use you as a weapon for the Government while the Elector President takes over the world. Okay, here goes..."I wince a little bit, afraid to tell Cody the truth.

"The truth is...They put in panther DNA in our blood, so...We're growing ears!" I kind of chuckle nervously, and watch as Cody's tiny little panther ears wiggle.

Which explains why I have the hat on.

CHAPTER 42

"So...We're growing panther ears?" I ask cautiously.

"And tails," April whispers in response. "I'll explain more. They gave us panther DNA so we could be part of their army to take over the world. But this isn't just a normal panther. We can run up to 100 miles an hour without stopping, jump up more than ten feet, our flexibility is increased by 400 percent, our muscles are made to be even tougher, made to be lighter and differently so we can move around better, and we can climb trees or other tall structures up to 1,000 feet or more."

"Wait, I just have one question," I cut in. "It's about the ears. Since I'm growing cat ears, where are my human ears...?"

"You won't have human ears anymore," April answers kind of sadly. "But since we have these new panther ears, our hearing will increase by about 100 percent. We will also have a better sense of smell, which means that all of our five senses are going to be improved much better. Which means that we are going to be stronger than an average grown man, or a few average grown men."

"You're saying that as if it were a bad thing." I smirk. "Just think about how easy it would be to fight people, or, most important of all, to find the Generator, and save the world."

April stops. "Wait...Oh, my gosh! You're right! Maybe this is good!"

"This *is* good, April," I say matter-of-factly. "Now get me out of this cell before I die from claustrophobia."

April smiles. "Okay," she agrees. "Just one more thing to say. Keep your hair like that from now on, okay?"

I hesitantly reach up to tousle my jet-black shoulder-length hair. "Why?"

"Think about how creepy it would be for people to realize you don't have human ears. There'll just be skin there. I'll keep my hair down all the time, too, only occasionally pulling it up in a ponytail for fights and such, to keep it out of my face."

"You sure do talk a lot," I sigh. "Let's get out of here."

CHAPTER 43

⟨⁓⟩

Cody and I walk up to the front door of the Military Training Center, having both hats on, and Cody being in disguise. (We had to stop by at a party store, where he shook hands with some guy he called Jeff, and when Jeff asked him why he looked so different, he said he bleached his hair black and put in colored contacts to mess with his friends.)

The guards standing in front of the entrance looks down at me, and I show them my identification card. One guard nods, and opens the door for me and Cody.

Once we're farther down the hallway, Cody leans over to me and asks, "Where are we going?"

"Remember in my room at the school where we discussed our plans to get in the Government Building?" Cody nods in response. "Well, we're going to that old, abandoned, dirty, ugly, small printer room, and I've got matches."

Cody grins as if this were his favorite thing to do.

After going down hallway after hallway, I can tell that Cody is wondering how big the Training Center really is, because it probably took us about 15 minutes to get to where we were supposed to go.

I fish out some keys from my pocket and stick it in the lock, turning it and pushing open the door.

A cloud of dust greets me and Cody as we step in to see piles of old, moth eaten paper, a row of printers on falling-apart desks, and a skylight, which was the only light source in the ugly room.

"Ooh." Cody does a jogging lap around the room, examining it. "This is perfect for setting on fire. There are papers everywhere, which is even better. Since we can jump more than ten feet, the skylight's perfect."

"Yup," I reply, glancing up to the skylight. "The safest thing we can do is jump out of the skylight, and then set the room on fire."

Cody nods in approval. "Yeah, that's a good idea. Since we can jump up more than ten feet and climb stuff like a monkey, I agree."

"Do you want to go first?" I ask Cody nervously. The thought of being made like this kind of helps me feel better about this kind of thing, but I do not want to land in shattered glass.

"Yesssssss." Cody shoos me out of the way, which I do gladly, squeezes his eyes shut, and jumps.

Cody crashes through the glass as if it were paper and does a flip–I don't know if it's a cat thing–while grinning from ear to ear, and then landing with a *thud* on the roof. Glass showers all over me and I frown.

"Your turn," Cody calls down to me through the skylight. I nod slightly and stand in the the middle of the skylight where sunlight streams down onto me. I close my eyes, just like Cody did, and jump.

A whooshing of wind greets me as I jump high into the air, I donno, was it fifteen feet? Twenty feet? And I land perfectly beside Cody on my feet without falling on my face.

"See? Easy, right?" Cody says that to me as if he's done this a million times before. I scowl at him for a second before answering.

"Well, you're right. I could get used to this." I smile at him and Cody grins back.

"Okay, then. What are you waiting for? Light the place on fire!"

I slide out a box of old-fashioned matches from my jeans pocket– yes, *jeans pocket*. Just imagine how it was for me to jump up like that in *jeans*.

It takes me a couple of tries to get one match on fire, and I quickly throw it down through the skylight onto the floor full of old papers.

You will not believe how *fast* the room lights up on fire, and the fire alarm immediately goes off, but fortunately, Cody and I get out of there in time.

Time to go to the Government Building.

CHAPTER 44

April and I run at at least thirty miles an hour along the roof of the Training Center towards the Government Building, which, conveniently, is neighboring the Training Center.

It takes us less than ten seconds to get there, and when we do, there's only two guards in front of the entrance.

We crouch down low onto the roof to avoid being seen and April asks me, "Should we get them, or just ignore them and climb the Building?"

"What? How can we climb *that*?"

"We can climb 1,000 feet or more, remember? And we can take occasional break on the window ledges, since they're freaking huge."

I think this through for a moment. "Let's go on to climbing the Building. We need to get to the top ASAP. If anyone spots us taking breaks on the window ledges, we can vanish before their sight. We're supposed to be like ninjas, right?"

April nods. "Okay. Get up and do a running jump onto the highest ledge you can get. If the guards spot us, stay behind the frame. It's big enough to shield both of us. And we should climb separately to avoid crashing into each other."

"All right."

I stand up and get into a running stance, and I take off, jumping fifteen feet into the air and landing gracefully on the highest window

161

ledge I could manage to get to (the third floor, in case you were wondering).

Looking back, I realize that April is already gone, and is on the neighboring window ledge.

And we start to climb.

CHAPTER 45

We climb for a pretty long time, and by the time Cody wants to take a break, we're probably already at the 70th floor of the Building.

"Fine," I reply. "If we keep going on like this after the break, we'll get to the top in no time."

"Right," Cody says and lies down on the windowsill. "But I just have one question. How are we going to get inside once we get up there?"

I pause. In my dream I had in Cody's coma, I was the Elector, and his office didn't have any windows. So that completely changes things.

"I don't really...Know," I begin slowly. "Maybe there's a hatch or something at the top, on the roof."

"Oh," Cody sighs. "Well, then, we're doomed."

"Damn," I mutter under my breath.

"Say what now?" Cody asks me suspiciously.

"Nothing," I mutter in response. "Let's just keep going."

"But waaaaaiiiit," Cody whines, "we just started the breeeeeaaaaak."

"We have to figure out how to get in when we get to the top. Therefore, we need to get going. And quit your whining."

"I have one more question. What did you just say?"

"Nothing."

"C'mon! Tell me!"

"You don't understand. You're still a child."

"I am not!"

"Well, you're acting like it."

"Hmph!"

We stand on our windowsills in silence for a second, the only sound we hear is the distant sound of aircars passing by on the road. *Seventy floors down.*

"Um, let's go…" I start to grab onto the next window ledge and I pull myself onto it, knowing that I don't need to worry about falling.

Cody climbs up after me, and I let out a breath that I didn't know I was holding. I guess all the stress about getting inside is really getting to me. But I have to let the stress get to me only when we get to the top.

Ten minutes later, Cody and I have finally made it to the 99th floor of the Government Building, and we actually made it without Cody trying to flirt with me. (*winks creepily*)

"Can we take another break?" Cody asks abruptly, breaking the sweet, sweet silence I had for ten minutes. And Cody says that I talk a lot. I don't talk a lot, I like to inform people about things they don't know about.

"No," I snap. "We're almost there. You can rest at the top while I kick ass inside."

Cody lets out a breath. "But I want to go with you. Pleeeaaaase rest with me."

"No. We need to get inside as soon as we can. Or you can just rest while I try to figure out how to get inside."

"Well, okay. At least I could rest. I'm tired."

"C'mon, let's go." I gesture towards the top and start to climb the remaining windows of the Building.

At the top, the wind blows against me very harshly, as if it wants to tip me over. But a normal man wouldn't even be able to stand in this wind. There isn't a fence around the perimeter of the roof, so I guess no one is meant to be up here.

I look over the edge.

There is a magnificent view of the entire city. Tiny aircars rush by looking like ants. Don't even get me started on the people. I can barely see them.

"Maybe nobody's not supposed to be here 'cause the air is so thin. But I'm breathing fine." The sudden voice startles me, making me jump. I never noticed Cody coming up.

"Yeah, that's because we have bigger lungs, and they're stronger, so since we can climb such tall structures, we can get oxygen from thin air."

"Huh." Cody comes over to me and looks over the edge. "Whoa. What a view. If I could fly, I would be happy to jump off of this building and just start flying. Or I could get a squirrel suit. That would be awesome."

"I agree," I begin, "but unless we get our asses in the Building, you won't be able to get a squirrel suit when we get out."

Cody makes an annoyed *tsk* sound. "You're saying that as if we *will* be able to get out under any circumstance."

I scowl at him. "I *know* we will get out, and we *will* get out, because I say so."

Cody laughs. "Just because you're the super smart prodigy girl of Government City, doesn't mean that you're always right."

"Ugh." I turn away and start to look for any entrances into the Government Building. Since we have way sharper eyesight, this is actually going to be easier.

"I'll take my break while you look, 'kay?" Cody doesn't wait for an answer, he immediately plops down against the edge of the roof.

I want to tell him that if we lies down like that, he'll fall over the edge, but I don't really care. I *should* care, but I'm way too into looking for an entrance than to actually care.

CHAPTER 46

I pretend to be asleep, but I'm actually listening to April mutter curses in different languages. It's actually pretty entertaining.

I can recognize only a few curses in some languages.

"Did ya find it yet?" I demand with one eye open. I can see April jump with surprise. Again.

"No," she answers. "Perhaps you're sitting on it? *Que la grasa perezoso.*"

"What?" I say in a rising tone annoyingly. "What did you say?" April grunts in response.

"Just get up," she orders.

She actually looks pretty scary commanding me to get off my butt and do something.

So I do what she says.

April crouches down and focuses on the spot I was sitting on. She fingers a crevice that I never noticed before and turns back to me, giving me a look.

"Like I said," she says, "*que la grasa perezoso.*" She feels the hatch for a moment while I stare and finally she pops it open. Warmth bursts in our faces and I shiver, finally being able to find someplace warm.

"Oh, yes. So warm." I close my eyes for a moment and crouch down next to April. When I open my eyes again, she's gone.

"Come on!" I hear April shout from down the hatch. "And close the trapdoor on your way in!"

"'Kay." I jump down into the warm Building, grabbing onto the edge of the hatch and slamming it shut.

Surprisingly, me slamming the latch shut wasn't loud at all. Maybe because it's new. Or something.

I land on a lush, royal red carpet in a long, long hallway. It's dimly litten, and there are portraits of past Electors of the Government.

This kind of feels like déjà vu. I wonder why.

"Now what?" I ask.

"We look, I guess," April replies casually. She starts walking down the hallway but trips and ends up on her knees. She curses yet *again*.

"Can you stop swearing already?" April looks up to me and gives me another nasty look. She gets back up.

"I'm sorry." She puts her hands up as if she were surrendering. "I'm just really stressed out, okay? All this 'saving the world' stuff is really getting to me."

"Okay, sure. I understand. Let's go."

April and I begin to tiptoe quietly down the hallway, which, by the way, have *no doors*. I wonder when we're going to meet one.

Ten minutes go by.

"I'm hungry," I whisper.

"Shh."

I roll my eyes and keep going. Another ten minutes past.

"No, seriously, I'm hungry," I say.

"Shut up."

Ten minutes again.

"Have you brought any food by any chance?" I ask.

"Oh, look. A door." April ignores me and gestures towards a dark red door. We're already at the end of the hallway. I never knew that hallways could be this long.

"Do you think it took us that long because we tiptoed to the end of a freakishly large hallway?" I ask.

"No. I'm going in."

I roll my eyes again but stand by April and watch as she will make her very conspicuous attempt at getting inside a room that could be the Elector's office.

She grabs the doorknob and gulps, slowly opening the door and peeking inside.

"Hello?" she whispers. And I was like, *Great job, April! Way to be subtle!*

Suddenly April shuts the door. "Oh, crap," she says, "run."

I don't hesitate and turn around, starting to sprint at 30 miles per hour.

"Why couldn't we just run to the end of the hallway?" I shout at April as she catches up.

"Turn left!" she shouts back, ignoring my question. I sharply turn left to another long hallway, barely even skidding or sliding with my force.

We keep on running.

"Do you think we lost them?" I yell.

"Yeah. Let's stop," April answers and stops running abruptly.

To tell you the truth, I have no idea how that girl can just randomly stop sharply after running at 30 miles per hour. I have to run a little bit before slowing down, and then I have to jog back to April.

"What happened?" I ask as we both sit down in the middle of the hallway.

"I opened the door, and there was a meeting room, and, yes, with a meeting going on. All those people were guards." April lowers her voice to a whisper. "And I think one of them was Mascao." She frowns. "When he saw me, he kind of looked happy for a moment, and when he saw my cat ears, he just looked sad. Disappointed."

I pause. I have no idea what to say on things like this. "Oh, don't worry, he does love you, April. Don't worry"? Um, no.

"Um…" I stand up. "Should we continue looking?"

April wipes her eyes. "Okay." She also stands up and runs away down that hallway in the blink of an eye. I run after her.

We get to the end of the hallway after about ten seconds (with me almost crashing in the wall), and we see another dark red door.

"How many doors are there here?" I ask. We haven't seen not one door when we ran down the halls. Not one.

"Shush. I'm opening the door," April says whiling turning the door on the doorknob. She opens it and peeks inside. A light goes on as she does so.

April turns to me and grins.

"Is it it?" I ask, almost screaming with tension. "The office?"

"It's a small room with a desk and a shelf, and there aren't any windows. There's also a really loud rumbling noise," April answers. "I think this is it."

I jump up in joy and push April away a little bit to get inside the room.

"No one's here." I grin. "Get inside."

April obeys immediately and I slam the door behind her, closing the multiple lock that were on the door. Now this way no one gets in, except for the Elector, if he has the keys.

"Barricade the door," I order April and she nods, grabbing onto the desk and pushing it towards the door. I take a safe (that has nothing to do with this) and place it on top of the desk.

"Now we find the Generator," April says, literally hopping with excitement.

"Let's look under the rugs," I recommend. "There could be anything under these things." I make disgusted face at the patterns in the rugs. Who made these things? Five-year-olds?

April nods and crouches down, lifting up the edges of the rugs, then ripping them off of the floor completely, rolling them up and tossing them onto the desk barricading the door. I help with the other rugs.

"Nothing here," I say after scouring all the rugs (which is a lot) in the room. The desk is piled with rolled-up rugs. I perk up my ears a little bit and follow the sound.

"I think the sound is coming from the bookcase," April says. I guess she's been listening for the Generator too.

We both look at each other and nod, creeping towards the bookcase. The sound keeps getting louder and louder, and it makes me want to cover my ears, since me and April's hearing is increased by, like, 1,000,000 percent (or it feels like it).

"Get rid of all the books," April orders, and I don't even hesitate. I immediately begin to rip out all the books in the bookcase, with April doing the same.

Behind the books, I see some light coming through, and by the time we take out all the books, I realize it.

It's a room.

And in the room is the Generator, bigger than a car.

CHAPTER 47

M y mouth falls open as I stare at Cody in disbelief. "It's the–"

"Yeah." Cody cuts me off harshly and immediately starts climbing through one shelf.

"Wait." I climb through the shelf after Cody. "Shouldn't we hid the evidence?" I gestures towards the mass of books we made and the rugs piled up on the desk.

"Nah," Cody says. "By the time we do that, our hair would change to grey. Also, we can't take the desk out, can we?"

"No…" I mumble, hating to admit that Cody is right. I look up to see Cody gone from my side and at the foot of the Generator that supposedly runs the entire city. His hand runs over the sleek, grey texture of the surface and he whistles in approval. I jog over to him.

"So this is the great Generator, powering the entire city, inside and out?" I ask in annoyance. "There's no need to whistle in approval, Cody. This thing is *tiny*!"

"Tiny compared to every college you went to," Cody replies.

"But how can this thing power the entire city?"

"Science," Cody whispers, just barely enough for me to hear him over the rumbling of the Generator. He must be really impressed with this thing.

"Whatever. Let's just find the off switch and get the heck out of here."

"Okay." Cody starts to circle the Generator while I jump up in the air, landing on top of the Generator with a *thump*.

Let me just say that Cody and I are in a room with a piece of metal that powers the entire city, inside and out, while we have ears that can hear about 1,000 times better than our normal ears. And that is *pretty dang loud*.

I reach towards the place where my human ears used to be, and my heart skips a beat as I finger the smooth, earless area on my head. I let out a breath, letting my new cat ears twitch a little bit, and crouch down into a crawling position, scanning the top of the Generator for the switch.

"Nothing down here," I hear Cody call down below. "Can I join you?"

"Sure," I call back. I continue searching and hear another *thump* of Cody landing on the top of the Generator.

"They must've had some really good insurance," Cody says and chuckles. I don't know if I should chuckle back. I don't really feel happy, but I don't feel sad either.

"Ha ha…" I say awkwardly. "Is there even an off switch on this thing?" I add.

"If there's no switch on the top or on the sides to this thing, then, we're gonna have to…" Cody looks down at the Generator.

"Oh, no," I gasp. "Oh, no. We could explode."

"It's worth a shot."

"Why did we have to be chosen to be Disparate anyway?" I mumble, changing the subject abruptly.

"You have a knife?" Cody asks.

"Yeah, I have a dagger in a sheath in my pocket…" I stop. "Wait, no! This is dangerous!"

"…Says the girl who just climbed 100 stories of the world's tallest building and yelled at me to not take breaks."

Well, can't argue with that. "Ugh. Here you go." I stick my hand in my jeans' pocket and take out an old sheath containing a really sharp dagger that I just sharpened not long ago.

"Thanks." Cody grins and slips out the dagger with a *shing!* and readies himself, making a fist around the handle of the dagger.

"Wait, wait! Let me get off." I get up and hop off of the Generator, landing almost without a sound, swishing my tail proudly through the newly made hole in my jeans.

"Pfft." I turn around to face Cody hiding his face with a smile, shaking his own tail. I cross my arms and wait for him to do his thing.

"Alright, let's do this," Cody says, and stabs into the Generator, hard.

I squish my eyes shut and cover my ears, curling up into a ball and bracing myself for an explosion. I keep thinking to myself, *You're gonna die trying to save the world you're gonna die trying to save the world you're gonna die trying to save the world.*

But there's no explosion.

Carefully, I open my eyes and look up, still curled up in a ball and covering my ears.

All I see is Cody viciously cutting into the Generator with a smirk of triumph on his face. I take down my hands from my ears.

"No explosion?" I ask. Cody looks over to me with a look that says, *No duh.*

"Well, we're still here, right?" he says with an obvious tone in his voice. I roll my eyes and get up, jogging back over to the Generator and hopping on top of it, joining Cody as he continues slicing a large hole big enough for one of us to jump in.

"Do you go on or do I…?" I make a confused face and point to myself.

"I'll go in," Cody says, sliding the dagger back in its sheath. "I have a lot of experience with this stuff."

I cough a little. "Um, hello? Child prodigy here?"

Cody looks at me, handing me the sheath and gives me another look that says, *I don't care just go with it.* I don't go on.

He hops inside the hole, with me waiting on top of the Generator. I hear a little bit of clinking of metal hitting metal, and I peer inside.

"You okay down there?" I ask.

"Yes. Don't come down. I'm fine."

I watch Cody shifting through some wires and touches a little grey box fixed to the wall of the inside of the Generator.

"Is that it?" I ask again.

"I think. I'm gonna try it," Cody replies, prying open the box. There's a little light switch there, and for a second I'm surprised that the people who built this place made the on/off switch for the Generator so old-fashioned.

"It's because they built the city long ago, in 2017," Cody answers my question that I had *inside my head and I never said it out loud.*

"What?"

Cody looks out from inside the Generator. "Wait, did you say something?"

"No," I reply. "I was thinking about why they used this old-fashioned light switch in the Generator."

Cody pauses, his mouth open in shock. "Wait, so that means... I can read minds." I join his party of surprise by raising my eyebrows as I watch Cody lean against the switch in deep thought.

And the whole world goes dark.

CHAPTER 48

"You got a flashlight?" I ask from inside the Generator.

"No..." I hear April's voice squeak from above. "Do you?"

"Which is why I asked you," I reply, "I don't have one."

"Maybe we can feel our way out."

"Good idea. You better get out of the way. I'm gonna jump out."

I hear the thump of April hitting the floor after jumping off of the Generator. Then I hear footsteps. I reach towards what I think is up--I can't tell whether I'm upside down or rightside-up--and feel the sharp edges of the jagged hole I cut with April's dagger. After making absolutely sure that I am in the middle of the hole I jump.

Blood rushes through my ears as I fly into the air and I suddenly feel myself falling. I point my feet towards what I think is the Generator, and I feel the sudden impact of the ground coming in contact with my feet. Thankfully, I don't fall over.

"I'm coming," I call out, reaching my arms out in front of me, groping for the edge.

I feel a rush a wind against my face, and before I know it, I'm down on the ground, face-down, with my arms still sprawled out in front of me.

"Oof!" I grunt as I pull myself up from the ground.

"Where are you?" April says, her voice echoing in the room.

"I said, I'm coming." I start to walk in the darkness, my arms out in front of me to prevent myself from crashing into the walls. "Keep making some noise so I can tell where you are." Almost immediately, April starts singing something that I can't recognize. I walk towards the sound.

The song gets louder and louder until I suddenly feel a person before my hands.

"Mayday! Mayday!" April shrieks, reaching for my face and slapping it, leaving it stinging.

"Ow, calm down. It's me." I rub my cheek feverishly and grab April's arm. "We need to look for the bookshelf."

I hear a rustling of clothes that I think is April nodding. "Right."

With me still gripping April's arm, we start to look for the exit by touching the wall and following it.

April gasps.

"What, what?" I ask.

"I feel it!" April pulls away from my arm and she disappears. I panic.

Relax, I'm in the office. Walk two more steps and reach to the right, I hear April think.

I obey and take two steps forward, touching the wall at the same time. My hand bumps against something, and I bring up my other hand and pull myself through the bookshelf. I feel April pull me inside.

"I got a flashlight," she declares, shining a bright flashlight in my face. I blink in surprise. "And I also found squirrel suits."

"How?" I say in a surprised tone.

"I found them in a closet, and I have to tell you, the Elector does *not* have a good sense of style. And did you know that he wears a wig? There's a box full of them inside there." April slings two disgustingly yellow suits over her shoulder. "Come on, let's get out of here. When we get into the hallway, I'm gonna turn off the flashlight so no one will notice us, and we'll just use our freakishly good senses to get out of here."

I raise my hand like a little elementary school student. "Can I put on the squirrel suit now?"

Hmm, maybe we should put them on now so we can just jump out a window in case we need to escape. Or maybe we can just get out of here through the trapdoor and put them on on the roof. But then how will we find the trapdoor? The Building is like a maze. I smirk as I listen to what April is thinking. I decide to surprise her by answering her question.

"Yeah, you're right, how will we find the trapdoor? The faster way is to put on the squirrel suits now and jump out a window if we need to. The slower way is to try to find the trapdoor with our cat-like senses. And, did you just notice that we have night vision?"

April blinks in surprise, and I don't know if it's because I can read minds, or that we have night vision.

"What?" April says in confusion.

"Turn off the flashlight."

April still stares at me, confused, and switches off the flashlight.

For a second it's pitch-black, and then I can see a little bit in the dark, and it's gradually getting lighter.

Finally, after a minute of waiting for our eyes to adjust in shock, April and I stare at each other in exasperation, and the funny thing is, we *can* stare at each other, because now our eyes adjusted completely so we can see as if it were daytime in the room.

"Whoa," April whispers.

"Yeah," I say in the same tone of voice as April's, "now let's get the heck out of here."

"Wait! We need to put on the squirrel suits."

"Oh, right. Then let's do just that and scram."

CHAPTER 49

Since Cody refused to change in the same room as me, he went back through the shelf and into the former Generator Room. I changed in the office.

The suits were actually surprisingly comfortable. They were a little big, but I used a rubber band to tie any excess squirrel suit to the side.

"I'm ready," I call out to Cody, who's still in the other room.

"Just a 'sec." I hear some soft rustling (that I can pick up with my awesomely good cat ears, thank you very much) and Cody pops back into the office, his suit almost good on him.

"You know, I was thinking," I start abruptly, "since we're part cat now, does that mean that we have nine lives?"

"Yes, I heard you." Cody rolls his eyes, and I have to remind myself that he can read minds, and now he's using his new skill as if he were a God. But he's *not.*

"But I don't believe in that stuff," Cody finishes. "But obviously I can tell that *you* do."

I scowl at him and start to move the safe we put on top of the desk we used to barricade the office door. I place it off to the side, trying not to think too badly about what could be inside the safe.

"Treasure, I think." I whirl around to see Cody flashing me one of his obnoxious smirks.

"Stop," is all I can say. I begin pushing the desk out of the way, flushing with anger, which actually helps a lot.

"You sure are strong, for a girl," Cody says. This makes me turn even more red.

"Shut up." I scowl even more and turn back around to face the door, unlocking all of the locks, opening it gently and motioning Cody to follow.

He does, which is a first, and he closes the door behind him.

"Should we run?" he whispers.

"Um, yes. And jump out the first window you see." Without notice, I take off at full speed (well, maybe not full speed, because then that would be over 250 miles per hour, and that would be just darn dangerous), all of my senses perked up just in case.

"Window up aheeeeaaaad," Cody suddenly calls out, and I spot a speck of light in the distance, which is slowly growing to be a large four-foot window that leads down to the Training Center.

I panic, because I've never jumped out of a window of a 100-story building to other small buildings below in a squirrel suit that might not possibly work. It could have a hole in it, or worse, it wouldn't even *be* a squirrel suit.

"Don't worry!" Cody yells. "If the squirrel suit doesn't work, just pray over and over and over that you'll grow wings and fly away!"

If I weren't panicking, I would chuckle, because how would I just be falling and God would suddenly use this moment to help me? What if He doesn't want to help me? What if He's busy helping other people? He is God, after all.

"Stop thinking about your religion! Just close your eyes when we get out and spread out your arms and legs!"

I do what Cody says and as I crash into the window, my entire body burning, I close my eyes and spread out my arms and legs.

I feel wind catch in the rubbery flaps of the suit and slowly open my eyes.

I'm flying.

My eyes water, but I don't care. I smile a little bit before I laugh out loud.

"I'm flying!" I cry out.

Yes, you are, a voice says in my mind.

"What? Who said that?" I scream.

Me. Cody. I found out that I'm telepathic, too.

What's next, telekinesis? I think to Cody. I can feel him smirk behind my back in response.

Maybe.

I frown. When would I discover a hidden talent? Cody's already discovered two.

I spiral down to the ground from the Government Building, steering by leaning my arms to the direction I want to go to.

"Soldiers!" Cody yells at me, trying to inch to my side. I brake a little bit my stretching my arms up to my head and stare down at the ground. It's still a little hard to see, but guards that are looking like ants to me are crowding all over the city, evacuating people from buildings and leading them to the Pairing Center, the second largest building in the city (beside the Government Building, of course).

The ground hurtles towards me, and I can feel my ears twitching, picking up the conversations of concerned people hundreds of feet away.

"What are those things flying up there?"

"They look like people."

"Maybe they're soldiers."

"Come on! We need to get to the Pairing Center."

"But I wanna see what happens."

"It's dangerous out here."

"Did the city shut down?"

"I'm scared."

I turn my head towards Cody. "Let's head out of the city where there's open space!"

"Okay!" Cody steers left, veering past tall buildings, and I follow him. We sped towards the plains of the outskirts of the city we have learned to never talk or think about. Punishment, Execution.

Soldiers ran after us as we continued to fly at full speed to the ground.

We passed through the Wall.

I look behind me to see the soldiers catching up with us, and I keep on flying, about five feet off the ground. I get to the ground, running to keep myself from falling, and I stop, turning around to look at the dark city, being in front of the sun, and having the Generator off. The mob of soldiers continue charging at us. Cody stands next to me, crossing his arms.

"Can I meow?" he asks suddenly. I stare at him, surprised.

"I don't know, I mean, we're not complete cats, we're part panther, I think we can roar--"

"Cody Dalton Vares and April Christina Ingalls!" a soldier's voice in a megaphone shouted at us. "You are under arrest! Put your hands up!"

I blinked. Was this some sort of new thing they said whenever someone was under arrest? What *is* under arrest anyway?

"What's that" is what I want to say, but then the Elector President himself emerges from the crowd.

"Hello," he says casually.

"What--" Cody begins, but the Elector put his hands up.

"I have many things to explain," he continues. "And many questions to answer. First off, the reason why I wanted to get rid of the Disparate was because you got into my plan. It was magnificent. No one in the world would have thought of this."

"Why are you telling us these things?" I demand.

"Well, you already know everything, so I ought to explain things to you," the Elector replies.

"My plan was to take over the world," he says, "and I knew that almost everyone in the city adored me, except for the Disparate. I wanted to get rid of them. You Disparate were immune to all of my serums, and I don't know why.

"So I decided to kill all of you, one by one, slowly, so people wouldn't be suspicious. It was agonizing."

I stare at him, wide-eyed. "But if I was Disparate since I was a little kid, and Mascao was pretending to be Disparate, then why did you decide to kill him and not me?"

The Elector smiles. "April, the reason why I decided to get rid of just Captain Mascao, is because I am your father."

CHAPTER 50

W ell, didn't see that coming.

To make a long story short, April fainted. Right there. In front of the whole army, plus the Elector President, who just claimed him to be her father.

I feel like I'm in *Star Wars*, you know, on that part where Luke fights Darth Vader and he says that he's his father. That movie is old.

"What?" I say to the Elector, aka April's dad.

"Let me explain," he says. "April's brother, Mascao, isn't really her brother. He's been a spy--I like to call it babysitter--for my daughter all her life.

"When she was born, I decided that I wanted to rule the world, so I ran for Elector President. I wanted to start small before I go trying to take over the world. I won, or course, and I knew that April was going to be Disparate, so I put the Disparate tattoo on Mascao to fool her. The reason why I knew that April was going to be Disparate was because...Well, I am Disparate."

I gasp. "That's il*legal.*" I can see the Elector roll his eyes at me, and I smirk.

"The second things is that I can shapeshift," he continues, smiling at me. I almost fall over, but, frankly, I do not believe the little craphole (sorry for my language, everybody).

"Prove it," I order him. The Elector just keeps on smiling at me and snaps his fingers.

And he shapeshifts.

He shapeshifts into that guy that was in my dream three years ago while I was in the coma and inside my house.

He's James.

I almost fainted, too. But if I fainted, April and I would just be a big heap of fainted person, and the army would capture us, put us into jail, and we would be back at square one.

So I kept strong.

"Wh--what?" I ask stupidly. He smiles yet *again.* Except his smile in this form is a lot less attractive (NOT THAT I'M GAY OR ANYTHING HAHAHAHAHA).

"Yes, Cody. I was that man in your dream while you were in your coma."

"Then, what are you? Wait, let me guess, half...cameleon?"

James nods. "You're right. Except that I can not only change color, but change shape and size, too."

I try to act cool about this, but it's obviously not working.

"WAIT A MINUTE. HOW DID YOU GET INTO MY DREAM IN MY DREAM?!" I shout, still cradling April in my arms.

This time James frowns. "I'm afraid you are going to have to figure that out yourself, Cody." My reaction was just, WTH?

"Well, I'm afraid that I don't feel like figuring out anything else," I snap, "I'm tired, and sick of all you people."

James smiles again. "Oh, Cody, Cody, Cody."

I shiver.

"Don't you realize that you haven't figured out life itself yet?" he asks. "You have to go with the flow and try to find out."

Why is the Elector talking all riddly and mysteriously and stuff?! I'm already ticked and stressed out, why is the Elector trying to get into my brain?

But I can get into *his* brain.

I smirk mischieviously (as I always do) and try to tap into his thoughts. Maybe then I would be able to "figure out" life or whatever.

Then...

Nothing.

I get *absolutely nothing* from his brain. I can't feel his emotions. I can't listen to his thoughts. I try sending him something from my mind to his.

I get no response.

"You're a robot," I say.

He smiles yet *again.* "Well, you've figured me out. I guess I'm going to have to send you off somewhere else before you tell somebody else, or, the *world.* Goodbye, Cody." The Elector snaps his fingers and he disappears with a *poof* along with the army, and the entire city.

Or maybe it was us who disappeared.

EPILOGUE

April wakes up and groans. She was having a really bad dream about finding out that the Elector, the dictator of the Government City, has just claimed that he was her father.

She reaches to her side to feel grass. Was she sleeping on the ground? Where was she?

April opens her eyes and sits up, rubbing her face. There's another sleeping figure on the ground next to her. She spots a cat ear on the top of the sleeping person's head and realizes that it's Cody. She decides not to wake him up and stands up, scanning her surroundings.

Even with her cat like eyesight, she cannot see the city. There's only grass, and a couple of rocks and trees.

Now she decides to wake up Cody.

"Cody, wake up," she says, crouching down and nudging Cody's back. She hears a groan in response and smiles a little bit, starting to shake his back more.

"Cody, wake up wake up, where the heck are we?" April stands up again and unzips the flaps to her squirrel suit, revealing her arms. She brings out her foot and starts kicking Cody's back, gently. She hears another groan.

"Fine. I'm getting up." April brings her foot back down and watches Cody slowly stand up, wiping the sleep out of his eyes. He stares towards the sun rising in the distance, and then at April.

"Oh," he says. "I need to explain. When the Elector told you that he was your father, you fainted."

April's eyes go wide. So it wasn't a dream? She wants to faint again, but she decides to stay strong, especially in front of a boy.

"Then he sort of made us disappear, I guess? And now here we are." Cody finishes by clapping his hands together. "He said a lot of freaky stuff. And, did you know that he's a robot?"

April gasps. "My dad's a *robot*?"

Cody nods. "Apparently."

"So what do we do now?" April asks, and kicks a lone rock that was sitting at her feet. It bounces a couple of feet towards a tree.

"I have no idea." Cody sighs and runs a hand through his hair. "We need to figure out more about our world. We don't know where the city is on the planet Earth. So we should keep on going until we find people."

"That's a good idea," April agrees. "We should go east, since west is probably the direction of where the city is."

"How do you know that?"

"The sun sets west, Cody." April smiles. "When we were at the city, the sun was setting behind it. Therefore, we must go the other direction, towards the direction the sun is rising right now." She pulls up her sleeves a little bit more and, still smiling, runs off into the distance, with Cody following her as the sun keeps on rising higher and higher into the blue, blue sky.

CPSIA information can be obtained at www.ICGtesting.com
Printed in the USA
BVOW06s2326260715

410004BV00004B/31/P